visit us at
www.abdopublishing.com

Published by Magic Wagon, a division of the ABDO Publishing Group, 8000 West 78th Street, Edina, Minnesota 55439. Copyright © 2009 by Abdo Consulting Group, Inc. International copyrights reserved in all countries. All rights reserved. No part of this book may be reproduced in any form without written permission from the publisher.
Graphic Planet™ is a trademark and logo of Magic Wagon.

Printed in the United States.

Adapted by Vincent Goodwin
Illustrated by Cynthia Martin
Edited by Stephanie Hedlund and Rochelle Baltzer
Interior layout and design by Antarctic Press
Cover art by Cynthia Martin
Cover design by Neil Klinepier

Library of Congress Cataloging-in-Publication Data

Goodwin, Vincent
    William Shakespeare's Twelfth night / adapted by Vincent Goodwin; illustrated by Cynthia Martin.
       p. cm. -- (Graphic Shakespeare)
    Summary: Retells, in comic book format, Shakespeare's comedy about love at first sight, disguises, twins, and practical jokes.
    ISBN 978-1-60270-195-3
    1. Graphic novels. [1. Graphic novels. 2. Shakespeare, William, 1564-1616--Adaptations.] I. Martin, Cynthia, 1961- ill. II. Shakespeare, William, 1564-1616. Twelfth night. III. Title. IV. Title: Twelfth night.

PZ7.7.G66Wi 2008
741.5'973--dc22

                                       2008010747

Table of Contents

Cast of Characters

Viola
Twin sister of Sebastian

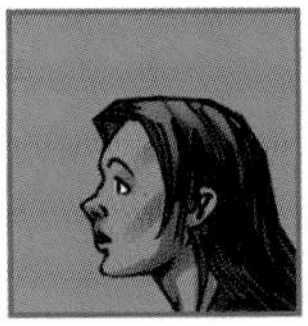

Cesario
Viola in disguise

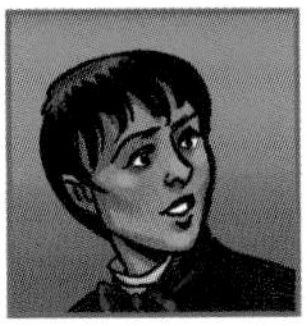

Duke Orsino
Ruler of Illyria

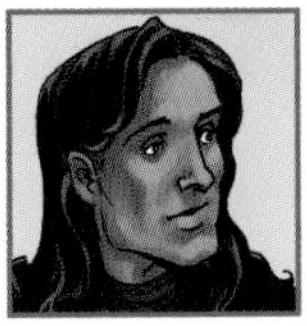

Countess Olivia
Lady of the house

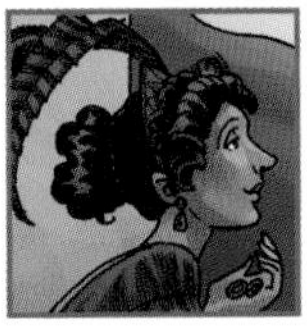

Sir Toby Belch
Uncle to Olivia

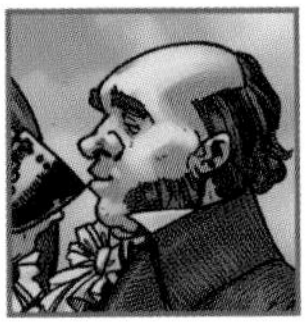

Sir Andrew Aguecheek
Friend to Sir Toby

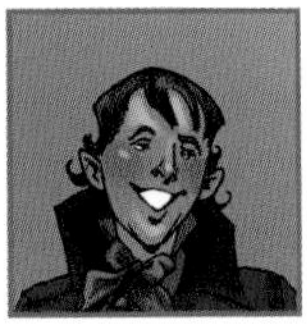

Antonio
Friend to Sebastian

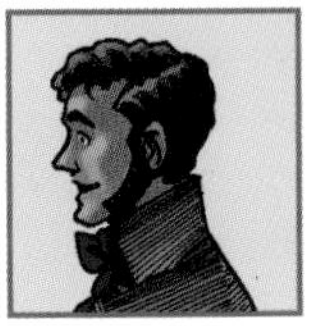

Mary
Olivia's servant

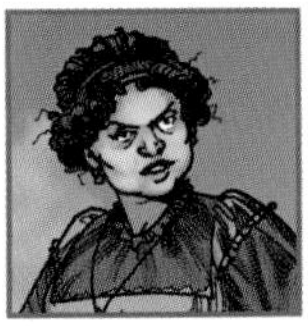

Malvolio
Steward to Olivia

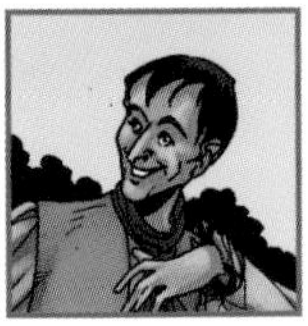

Sebastian
Twin brother of Viola

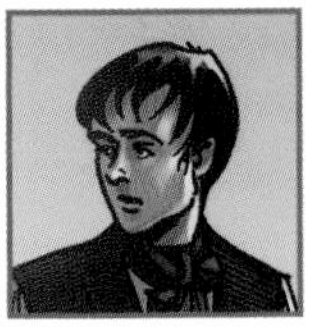

Our Setting

Twelfth Night is set in the mythical land of Illyria. However, Illyria was once a real kingdom. It was an ancient region in southern Europe. Present-day Albania now lies in its place.

The last Illyrian king surrendered in 168 BC to Roman rule. Several of the most well-known emperors of the late Roman Empire were Illyrian. In AD 395 the empire was divided. Over several centuries, with Roman impact, multiple cultures grew into a new Albanian population. As a result, the name Illyria gradually changed to Albania.

In the late Middle Ages, Albanian society prospered. This helped develop education and the arts. After many years of resistance, the Ottoman Turks began their occupation of Albania in 1506.

On November 28, 1912, the country declared independence. But communist rulers took control of Albania from 1944 until they were forced to resign in 1991. Currently, Albania is ruled by the Democratic Party.

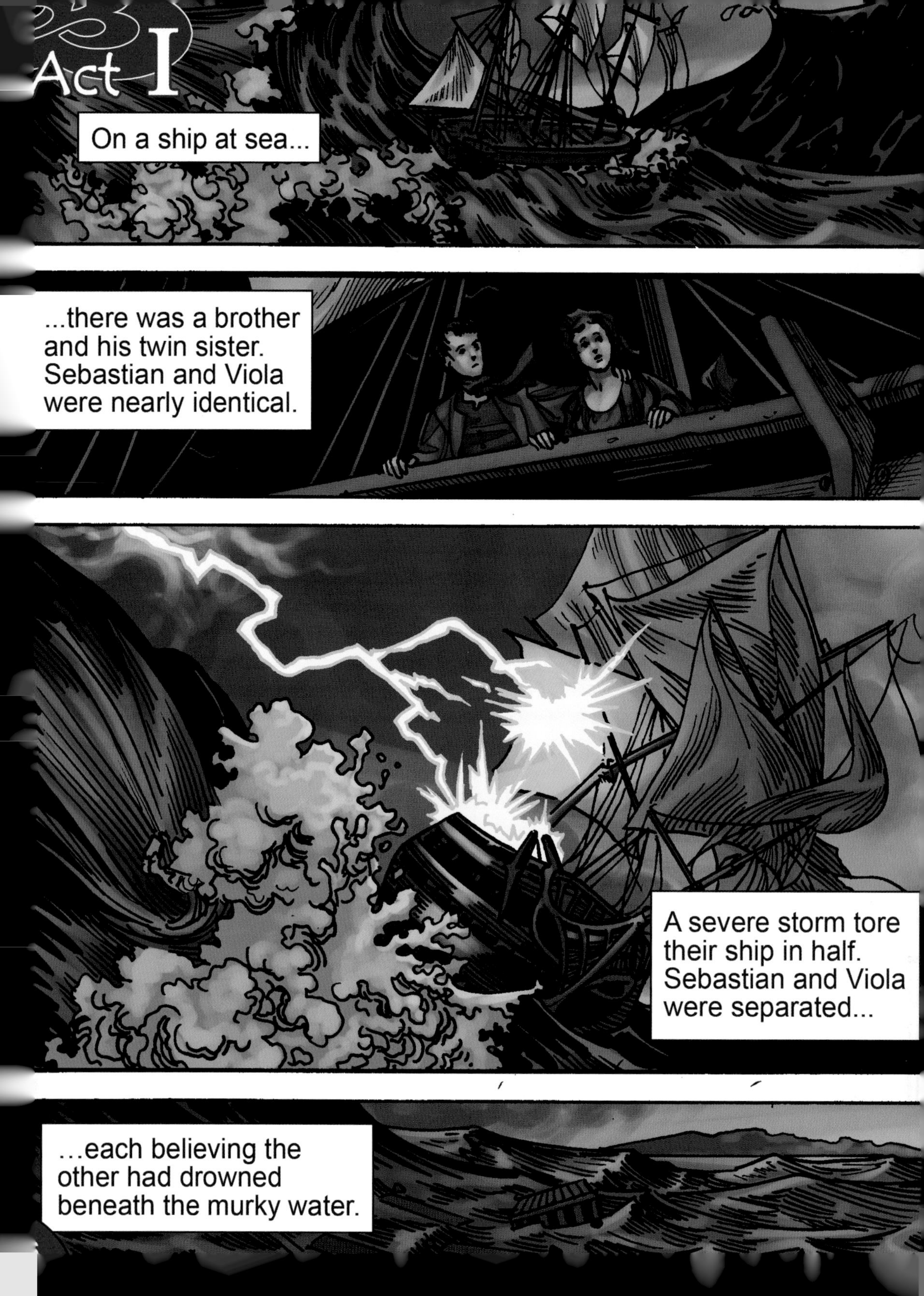
Act I
On a ship at sea...
...there was a brother and his twin sister. Sebastian and Viola were nearly identical.
A severe storm tore their ship in half. Sebastian and Viola were separated...
...each believing the other had drowned beneath the murky water.

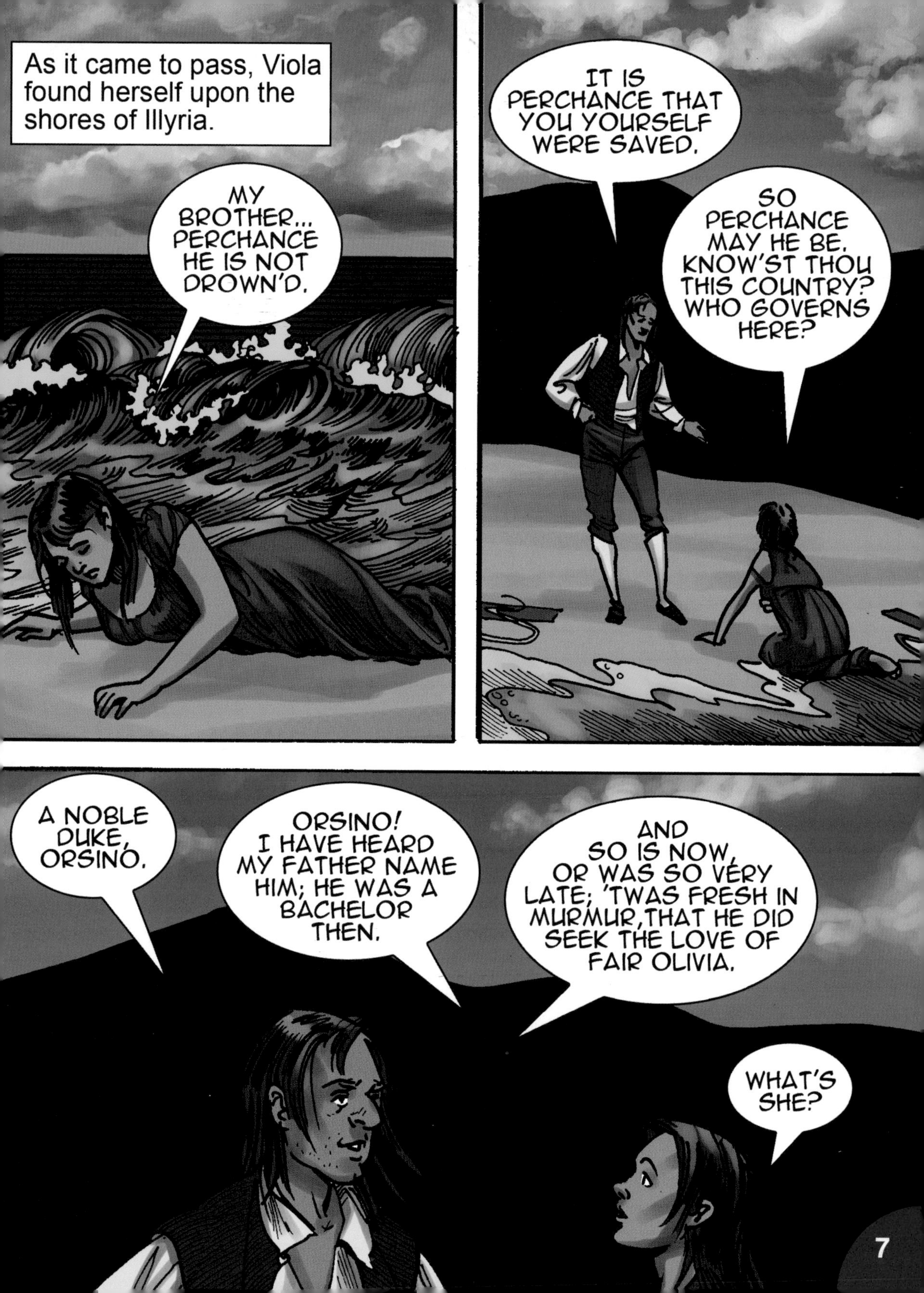
As it came to pass, Viola found herself upon the shores of Illyria.
MY BROTHER... PERCHANCE HE IS NOT DROWN'D.
IT IS PERCHANCE THAT YOU YOURSELF WERE SAVED.
SO PERCHANCE MAY HE BE. KNOW'ST THOU THIS COUNTRY? WHO GOVERNS HERE?
A NOBLE DUKE, ORSINO.
ORSINO! I HAVE HEARD MY FATHER NAME HIM; HE WAS A BACHELOR THEN.
AND SO IS NOW, OR WAS SO VERY LATE; 'TWAS FRESH IN MURMUR, THAT HE DID SEEK THE LOVE OF FAIR OLIVIA.
WHAT'S SHE?

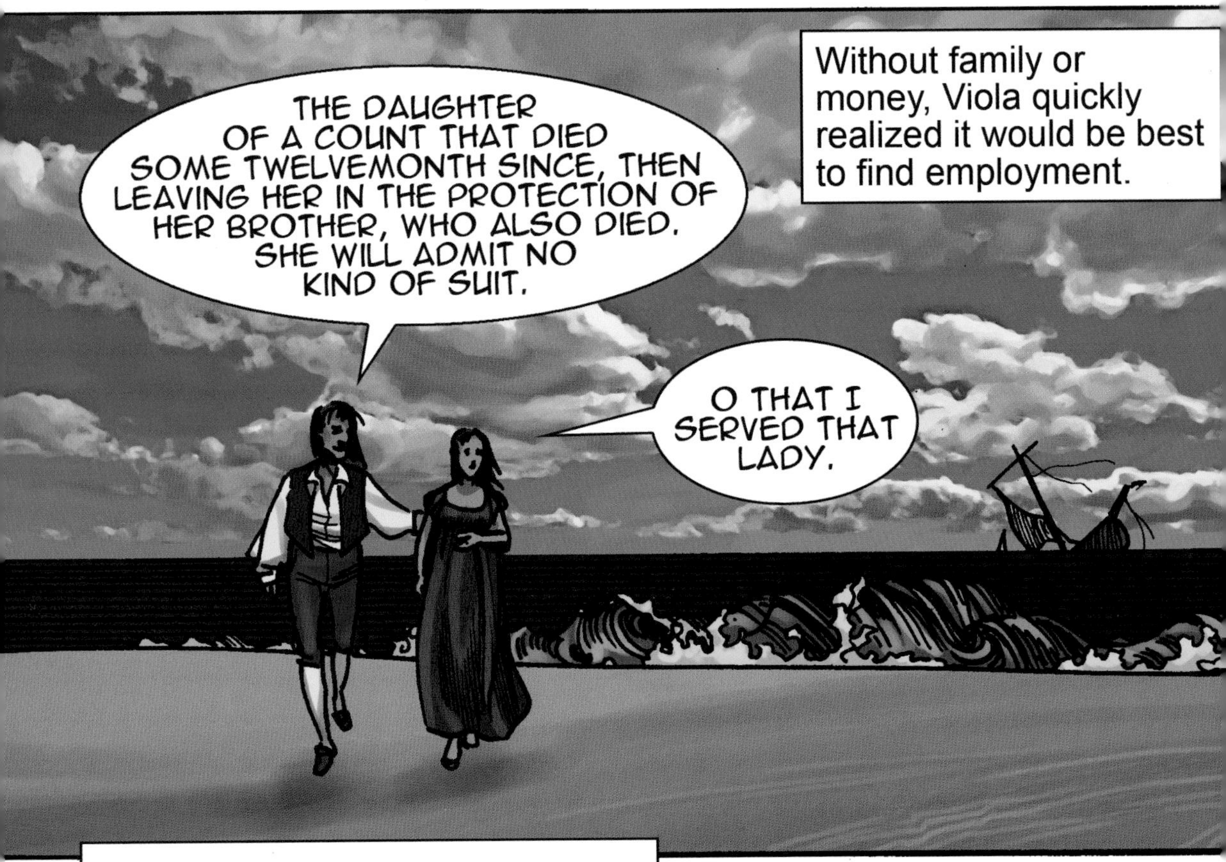
Without family or money, Viola quickly realized it would be best to find employment.
THE DAUGHTER OF A COUNT THAT DIED SOME TWELVEMONTH SINCE, THEN LEAVING HER IN THE PROTECTION OF HER BROTHER, WHO ALSO DIED. SHE WILL ADMIT NO KIND OF SUIT.
O THAT I SERVED THAT LADY.

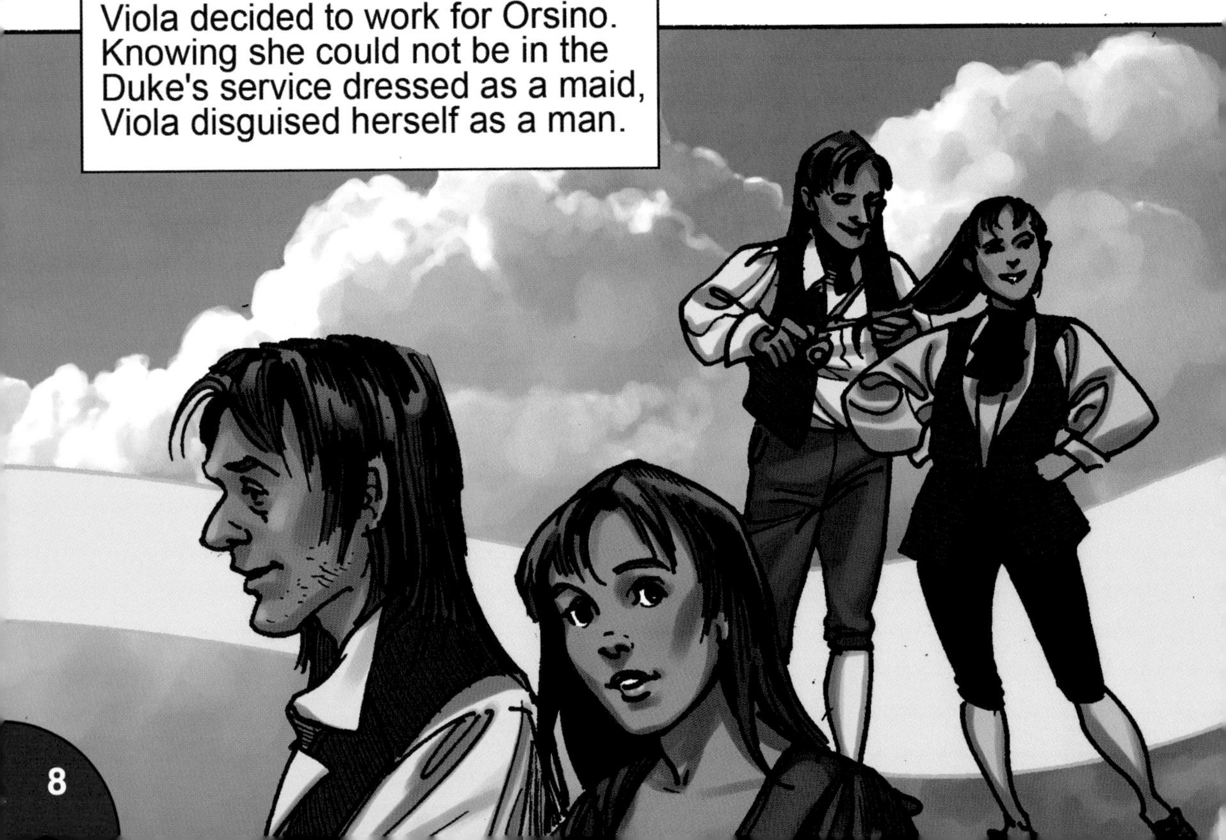
Viola decided to work for Orsino. Knowing she could not be in the Duke's service dressed as a maid, Viola disguised herself as a man.

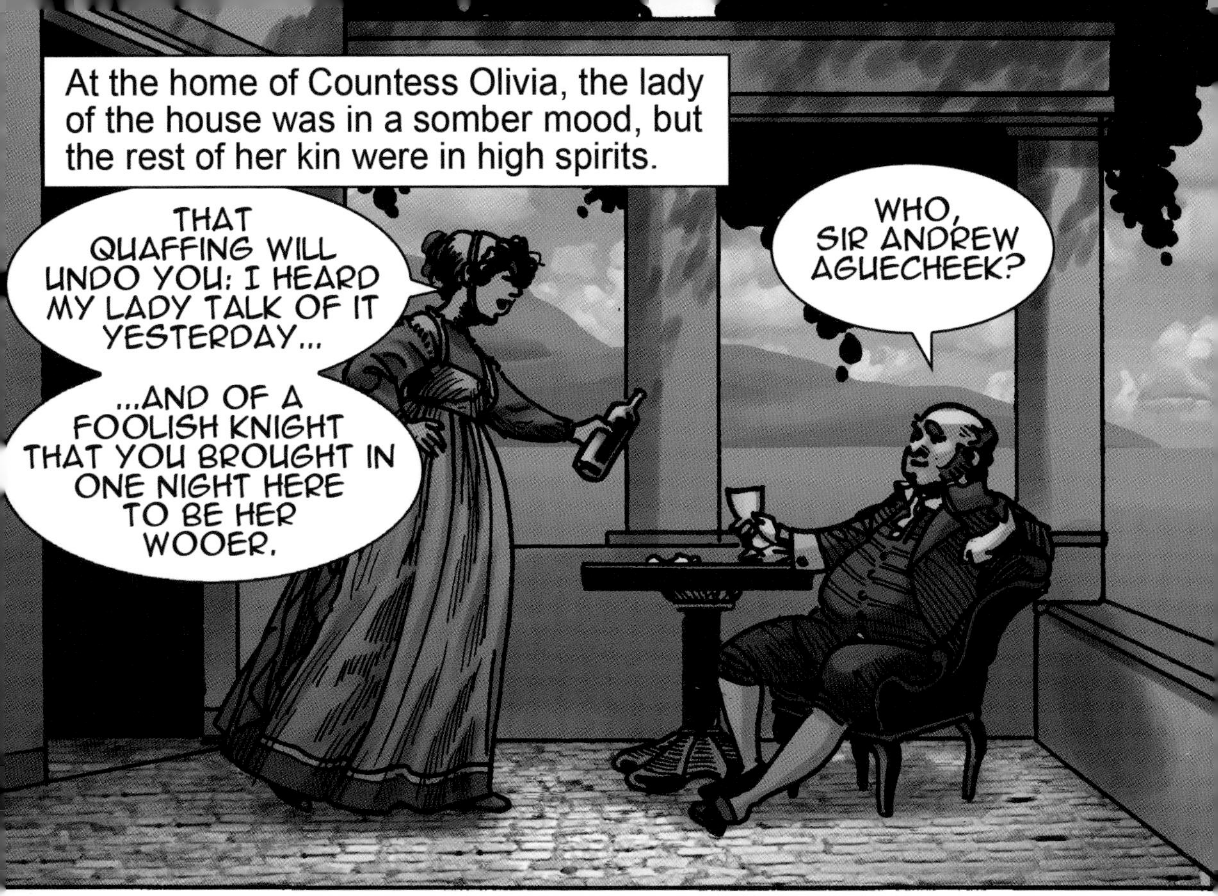
At the home of Countess Olivia, the lady of the house was in a somber mood, but the rest of her kin were in high spirits.
THAT QUAFFING WILL UNDO YOU: I HEARD MY LADY TALK OF IT YESTERDAY...
...AND OF A FOOLISH KNIGHT THAT YOU BROUGHT IN ONE NIGHT HERE TO BE HER WOOER.
WHO, SIR ANDREW AGUECHEEK?

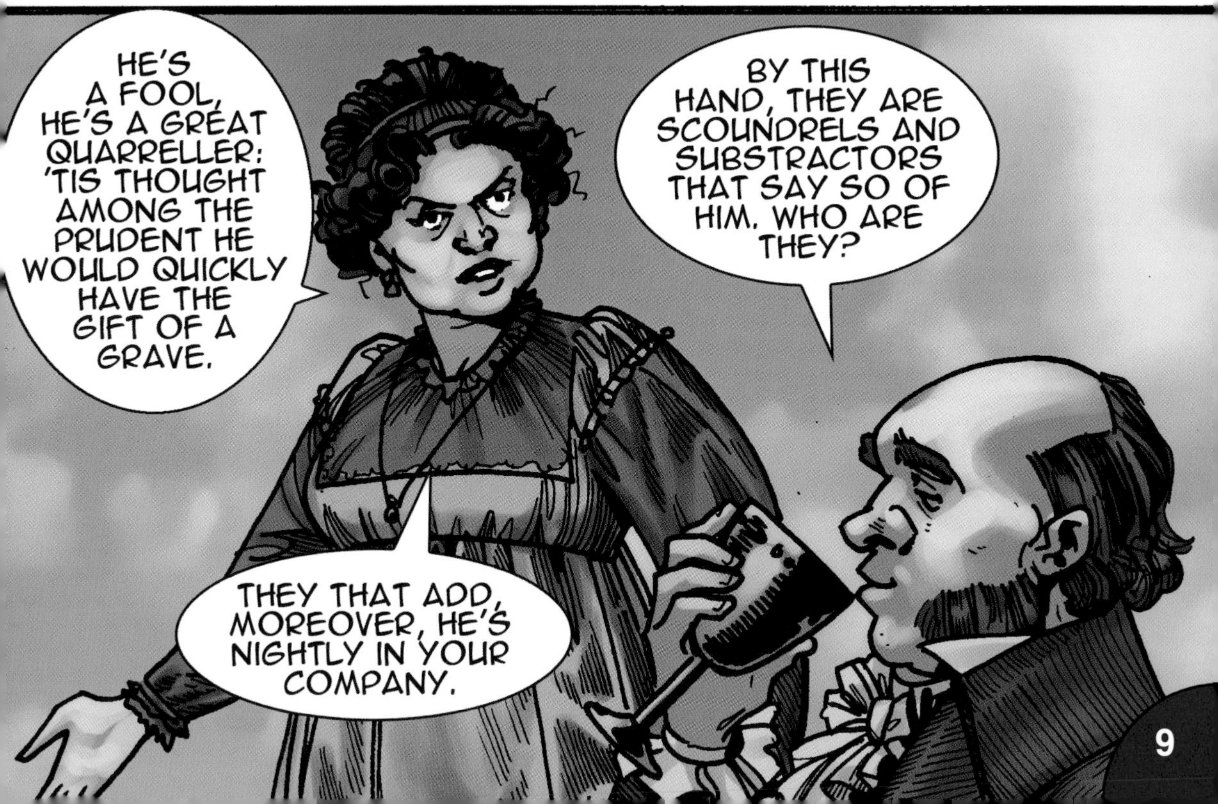
HE'S A FOOL, HE'S A GREAT QUARRELLER: 'TIS THOUGHT AMONG THE PRUDENT HE WOULD QUICKLY HAVE THE GIFT OF A GRAVE.
BY THIS HAND, THEY ARE SCOUNDRELS AND SUBSTRACTORS THAT SAY SO OF HIM. WHO ARE THEY?
THEY THAT ADD, MOREOVER, HE'S NIGHTLY IN YOUR COMPANY.

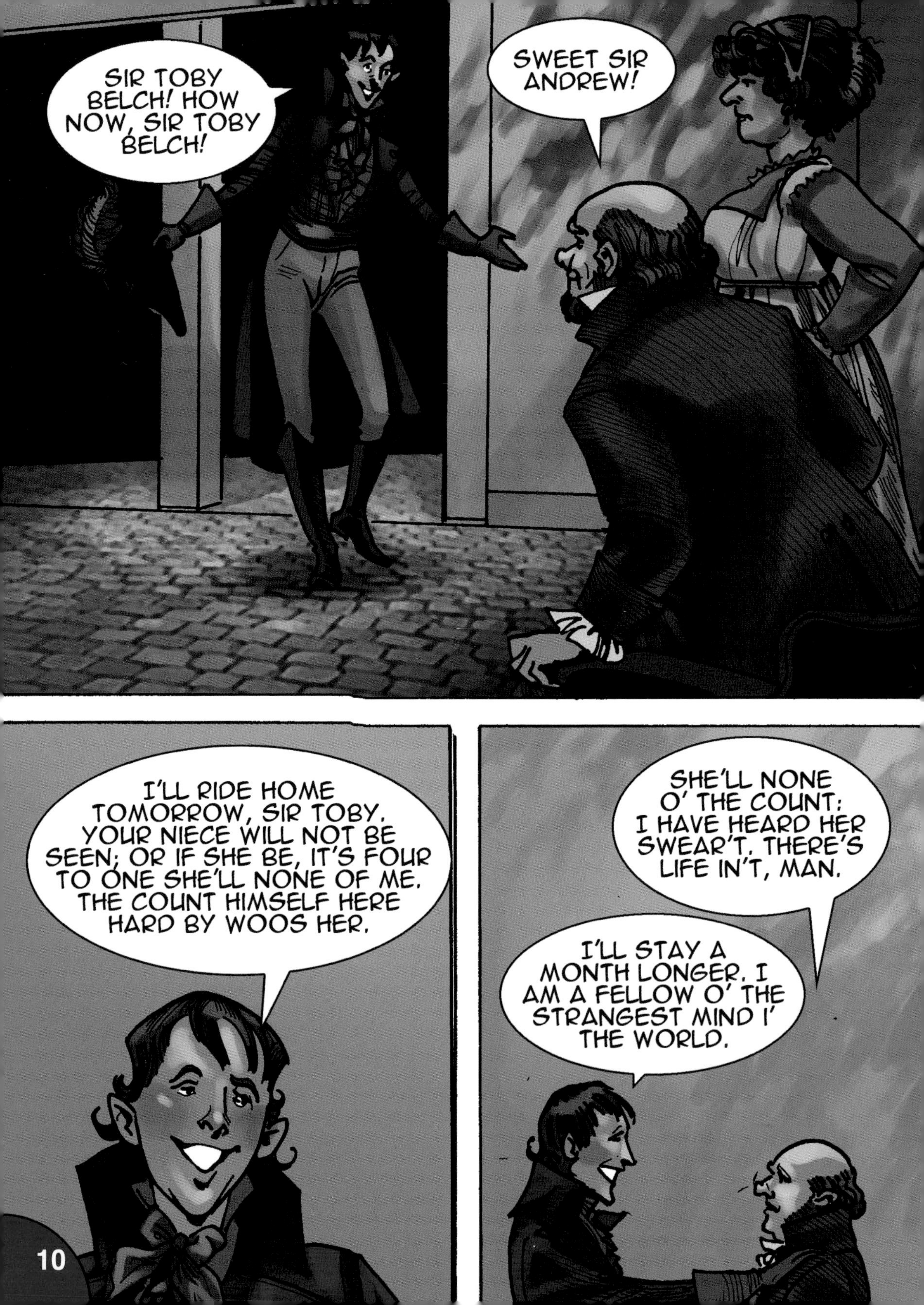
SIR TOBY BELCH! HOW NOW, SIR TOBY BELCH!
SWEET SIR ANDREW!
I'LL RIDE HOME TOMORROW, SIR TOBY. YOUR NIECE WILL NOT BE SEEN; OR IF SHE BE, IT'S FOUR TO ONE SHE'LL NONE OF ME. THE COUNT HIMSELF HERE HARD BY WOOS HER.
SHE'LL NONE O' THE COUNT: I HAVE HEARD HER SWEAR'T. THERE'S LIFE IN'T, MAN.
I'LL STAY A MONTH LONGER. I AM A FELLOW O' THE STRANGEST MIND I' THE WORLD.

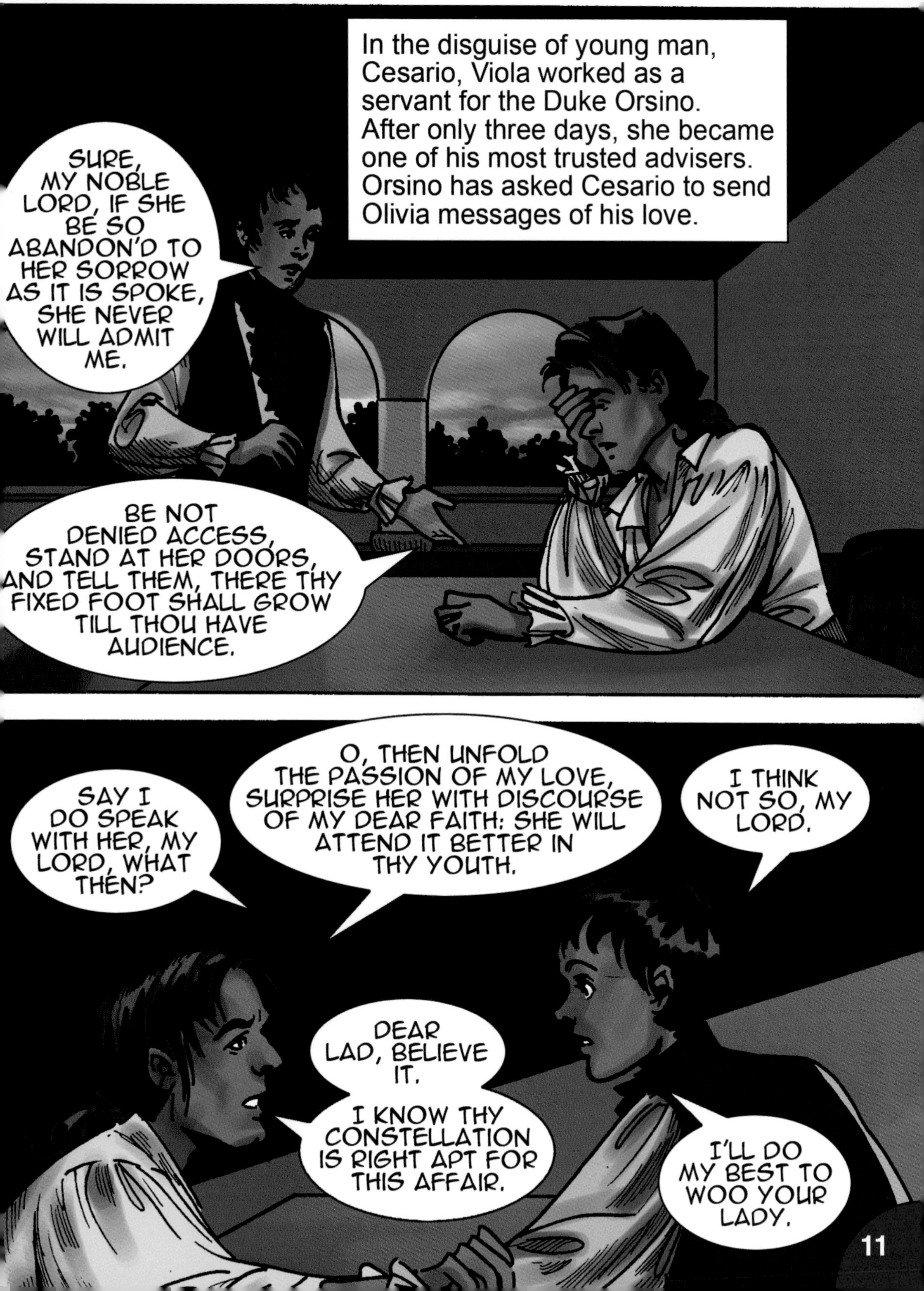
In the disguise of young man, Cesario, Viola worked as a servant for the Duke Orsino. After only three days, she became one of his most trusted advisers. Orsino has asked Cesario to send Olivia messages of his love.
SURE, MY NOBLE LORD, IF SHE BE SO ABANDON'D TO HER SORROW AS IT IS SPOKE, SHE NEVER WILL ADMIT ME.
BE NOT DENIED ACCESS, STAND AT HER DOORS, AND TELL THEM, THERE THY FIXED FOOT SHALL GROW TILL THOU HAVE AUDIENCE.
SAY I DO SPEAK WITH HER, MY LORD, WHAT THEN?
O, THEN UNFOLD THE PASSION OF MY LOVE, SURPRISE HER WITH DISCOURSE OF MY DEAR FAITH: SHE WILL ATTEND IT BETTER IN THY YOUTH.
I THINK NOT SO, MY LORD.
DEAR LAD, BELIEVE IT.
I KNOW THY CONSTELLATION IS RIGHT APT FOR THIS AFFAIR.
I'LL DO MY BEST TO WOO YOUR LADY.

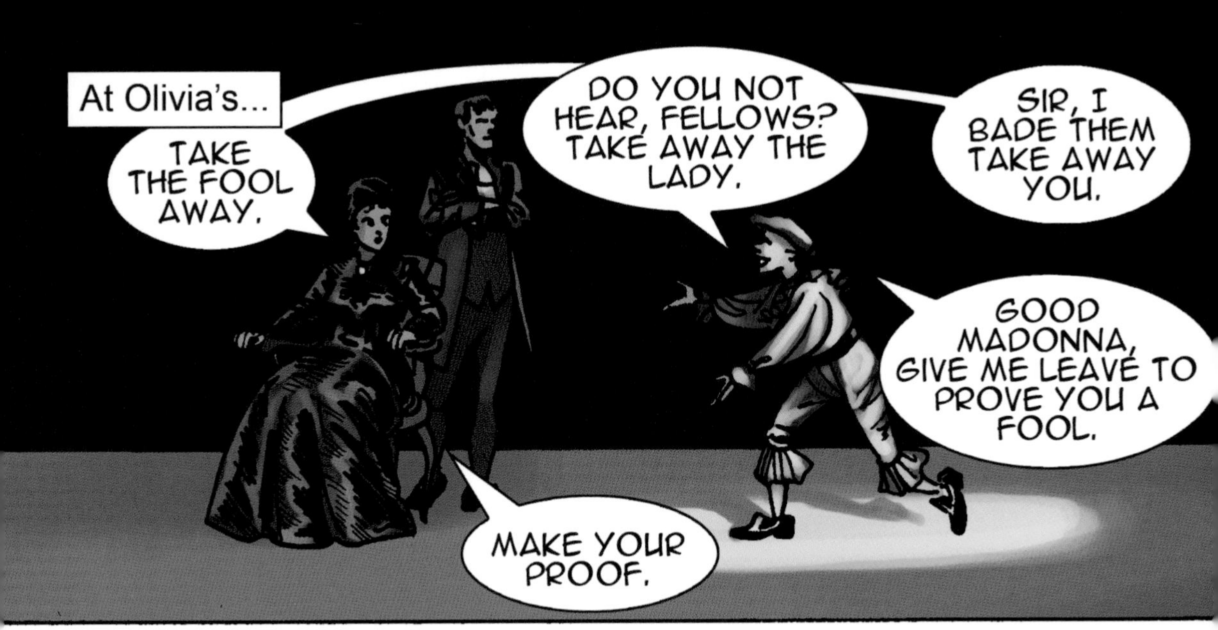
At Olivia's...
TAKE THE FOOL AWAY.
DO YOU NOT HEAR, FELLOWS? TAKE AWAY THE LADY.
SIR, I BADE THEM TAKE AWAY YOU.
GOOD MADONNA, GIVE ME LEAVE TO PROVE YOU A FOOL.
MAKE YOUR PROOF.

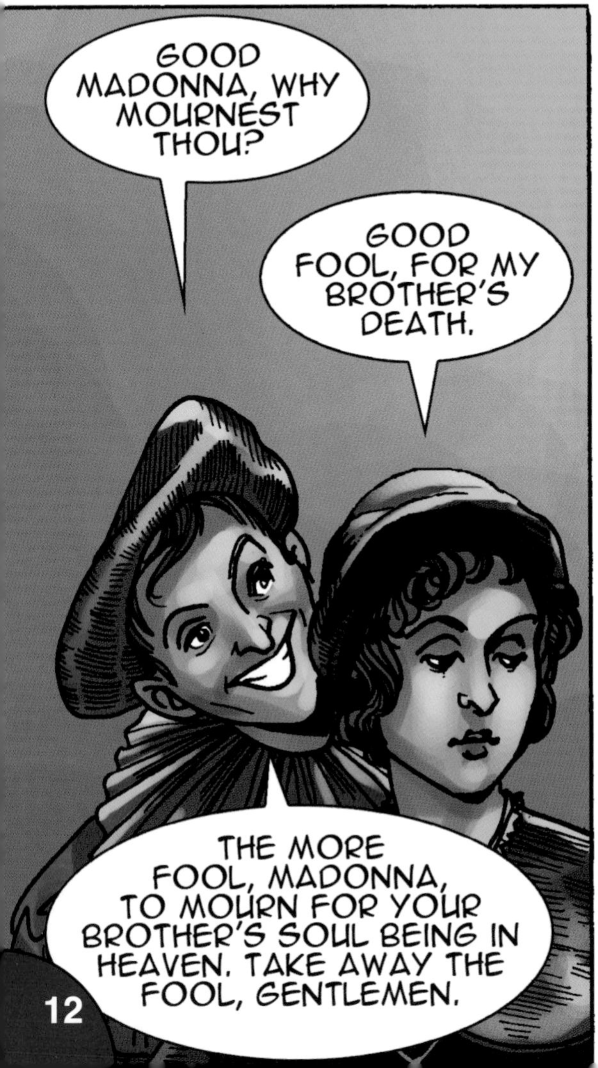
GOOD MADONNA, WHY MOURNEST THOU?
GOOD FOOL, FOR MY BROTHER'S DEATH.
THE MORE FOOL, MADONNA, TO MOURN FOR YOUR BROTHER'S SOUL BEING IN HEAVEN. TAKE AWAY THE FOOL, GENTLEMEN.

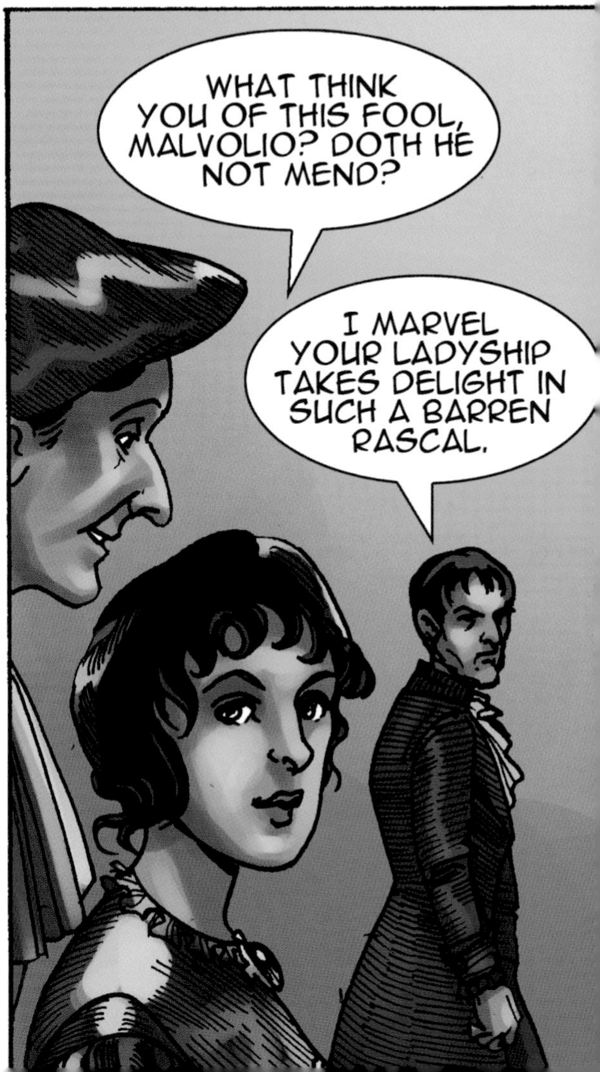
WHAT THINK YOU OF THIS FOOL, MALVOLIO? DOTH HE NOT MEND?
I MARVEL YOUR LADYSHIP TAKES DELIGHT IN SUCH A BARREN RASCAL.

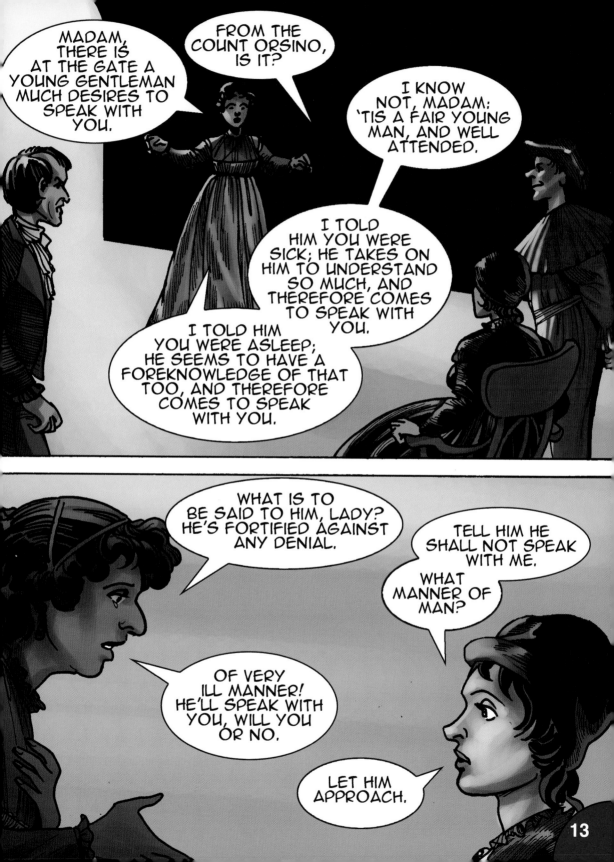

MADAM, THERE IS AT THE GATE A YOUNG GENTLEMAN MUCH DESIRES TO SPEAK WITH YOU.

FROM THE COUNT ORSINO, IS IT?

I KNOW NOT, MADAM: 'TIS A FAIR YOUNG MAN, AND WELL ATTENDED.

I TOLD HIM YOU WERE SICK; HE TAKES ON HIM TO UNDERSTAND SO MUCH, AND THEREFORE COMES TO SPEAK WITH YOU.

I TOLD HIM YOU WERE ASLEEP; HE SEEMS TO HAVE A FOREKNOWLEDGE OF THAT TOO, AND THEREFORE COMES TO SPEAK WITH YOU.

WHAT IS TO BE SAID TO HIM, LADY? HE'S FORTIFIED AGAINST ANY DENIAL.

TELL HIM HE SHALL NOT SPEAK WITH ME.

WHAT MANNER OF MAN?

OF VERY ILL MANNER! HE'LL SPEAK WITH YOU, WILL YOU OR NO.

LET HIM APPROACH.

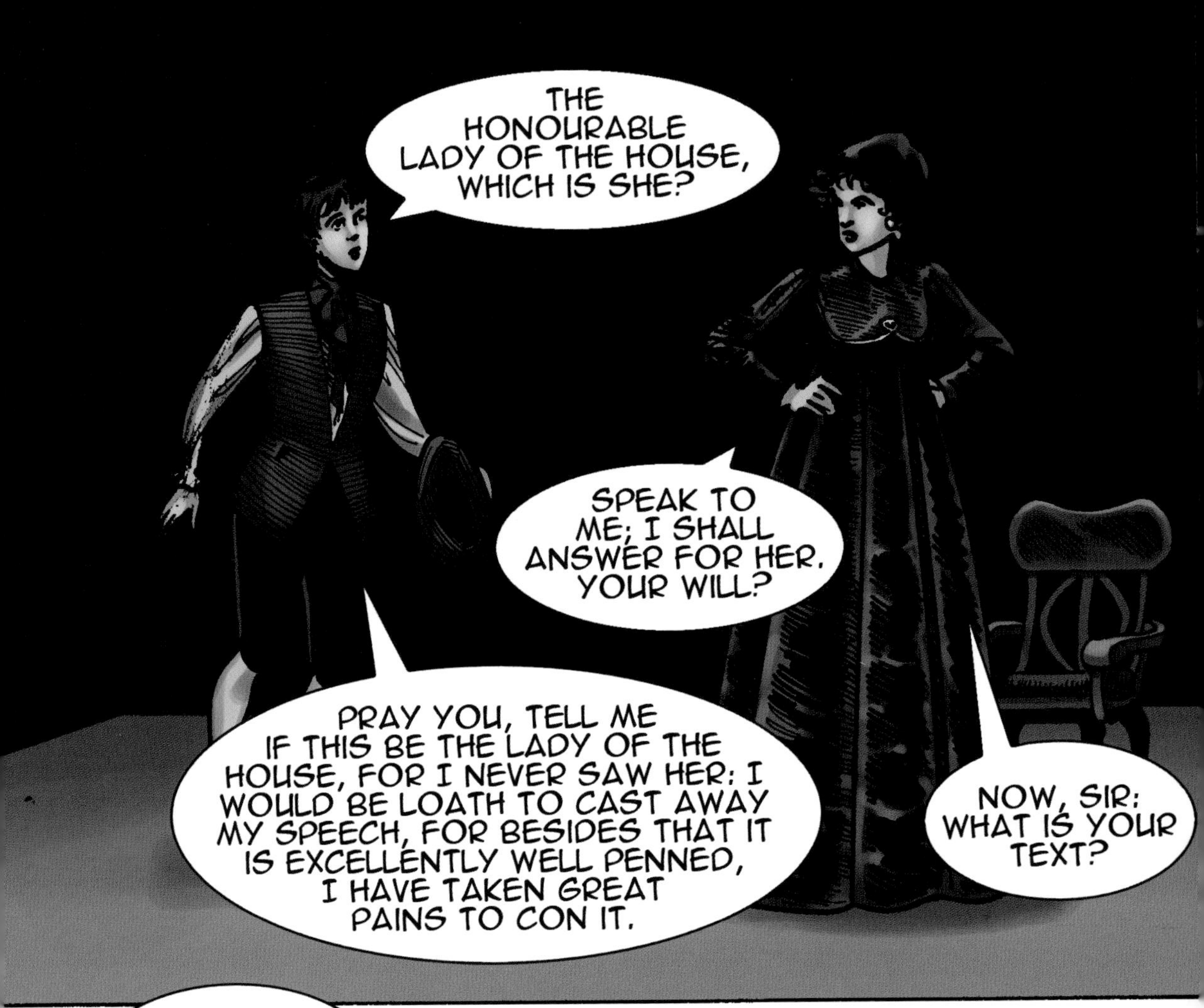
THE HONOURABLE LADY OF THE HOUSE, WHICH IS SHE?
SPEAK TO ME; I SHALL ANSWER FOR HER. YOUR WILL?
PRAY YOU, TELL ME IF THIS BE THE LADY OF THE HOUSE, FOR I NEVER SAW HER: I WOULD BE LOATH TO CAST AWAY MY SPEECH, FOR BESIDES THAT IT IS EXCELLENTLY WELL PENNED, I HAVE TAKEN GREAT PAINS TO CON IT.
NOW, SIR: WHAT IS YOUR TEXT?

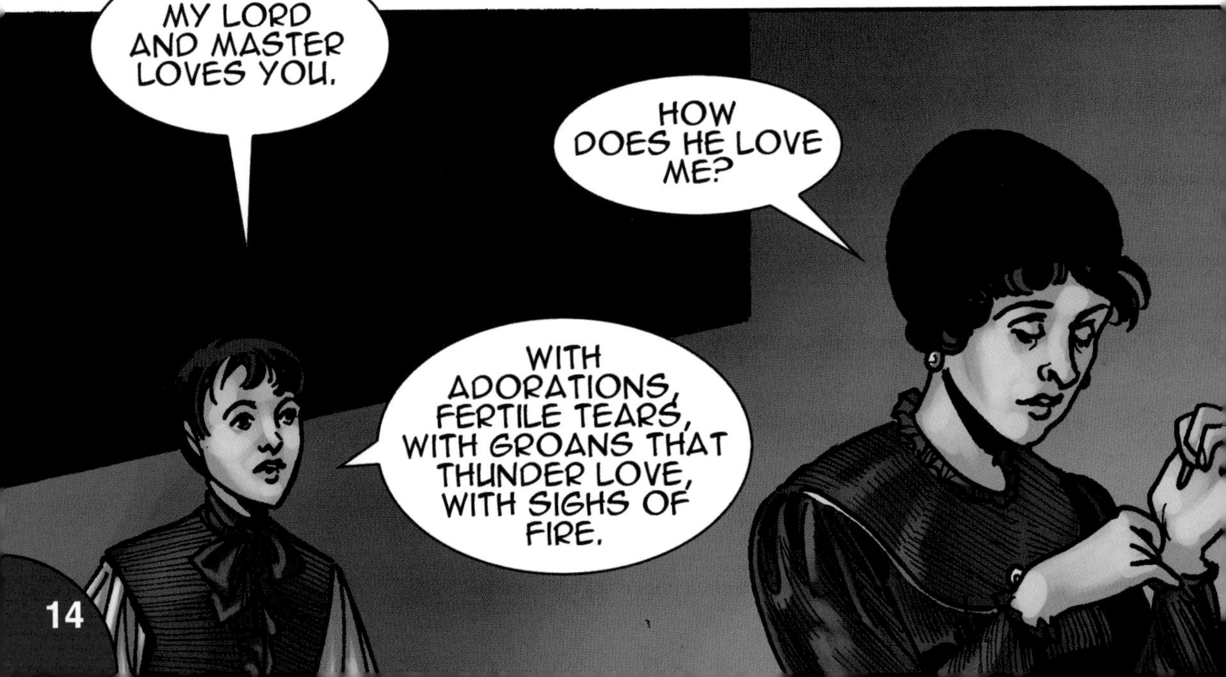
MY LORD AND MASTER LOVES YOU.
HOW DOES HE LOVE ME?
WITH ADORATIONS, FERTILE TEARS, WITH GROANS THAT THUNDER LOVE, WITH SIGHS OF FIRE.

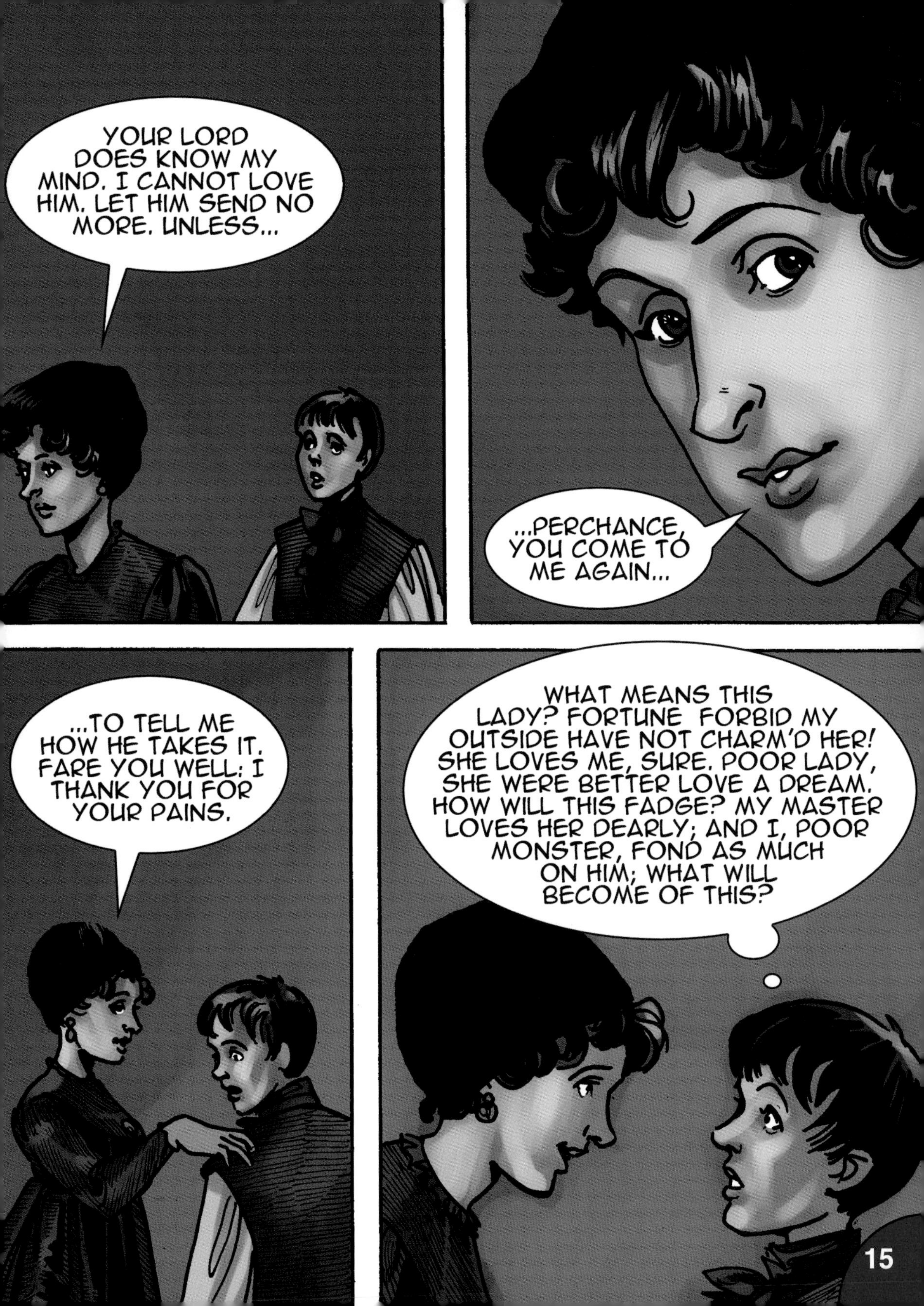
YOUR LORD DOES KNOW MY MIND. I CANNOT LOVE HIM. LET HIM SEND NO MORE. UNLESS...
...PERCHANCE, YOU COME TO ME AGAIN...
...TO TELL ME HOW HE TAKES IT. FARE YOU WELL: I THANK YOU FOR YOUR PAINS.
WHAT MEANS THIS LADY? FORTUNE FORBID MY OUTSIDE HAVE NOT CHARM'D HER! SHE LOVES ME, SURE. POOR LADY, SHE WERE BETTER LOVE A DREAM. HOW WILL THIS FADGE? MY MASTER LOVES HER DEARLY; AND I, POOR MONSTER, FOND AS MUCH ON HIM; WHAT WILL BECOME OF THIS?

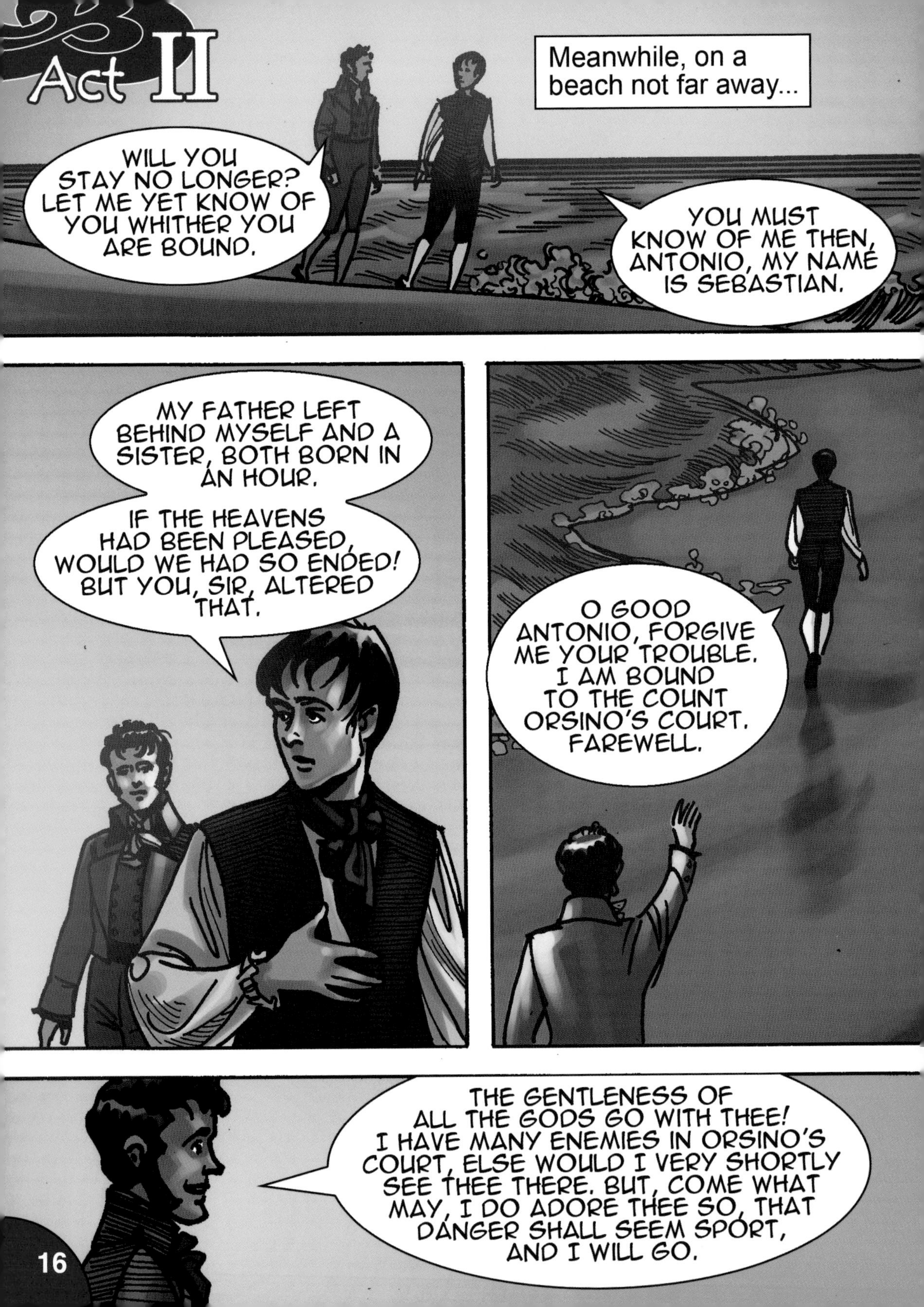
Act II
Meanwhile, on a beach not far away...
WILL YOU STAY NO LONGER? LET ME YET KNOW OF YOU WHITHER YOU ARE BOUND.
YOU MUST KNOW OF ME THEN, ANTONIO, MY NAME IS SEBASTIAN.
MY FATHER LEFT BEHIND MYSELF AND A SISTER, BOTH BORN IN AN HOUR.
IF THE HEAVENS HAD BEEN PLEASED, WOULD WE HAD SO ENDED! BUT YOU, SIR, ALTERED THAT.
O GOOD ANTONIO, FORGIVE ME YOUR TROUBLE. I AM BOUND TO THE COUNT ORSINO'S COURT. FAREWELL.
THE GENTLENESS OF ALL THE GODS GO WITH THEE! I HAVE MANY ENEMIES IN ORSINO'S COURT, ELSE WOULD I VERY SHORTLY SEE THEE THERE. BUT, COME WHAT MAY, I DO ADORE THEE SO, THAT DANGER SHALL SEEM SPORT, AND I WILL GO.

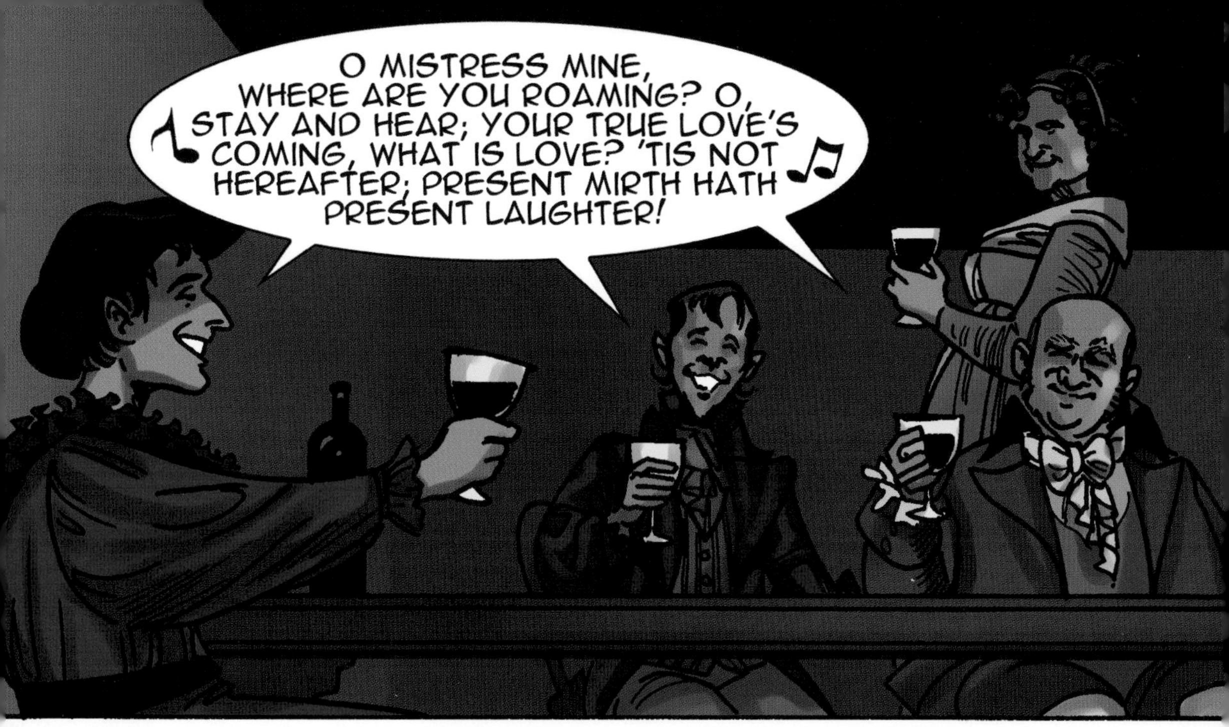
O MISTRESS MINE, WHERE ARE YOU ROAMING? O, STAY AND HEAR; YOUR TRUE LOVE'S COMING, WHAT IS LOVE? 'TIS NOT HEREAFTER; PRESENT MIRTH HATH PRESENT LAUGHTER!

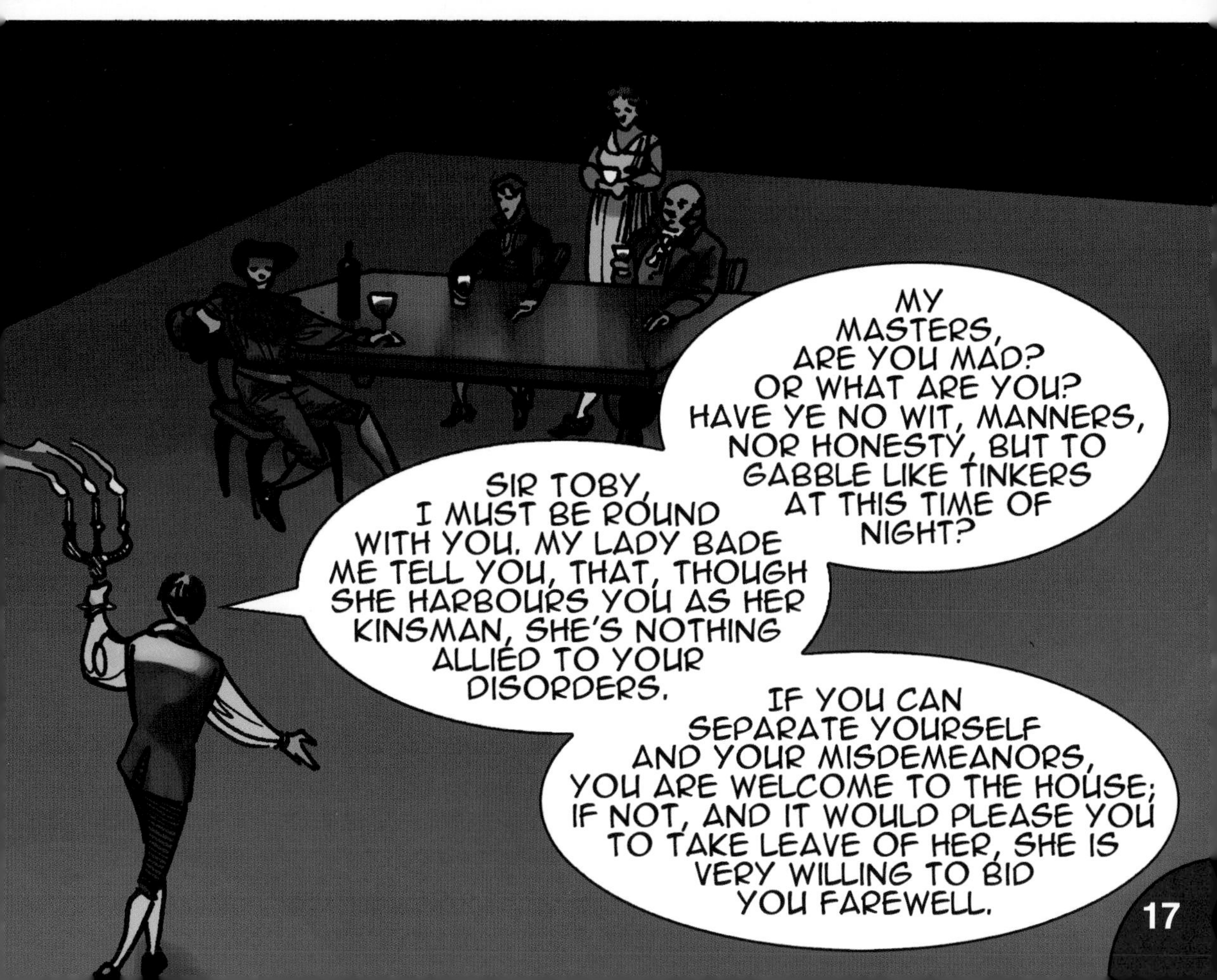
MY MASTERS, ARE YOU MAD? OR WHAT ARE YOU? HAVE YE NO WIT, MANNERS, NOR HONESTY, BUT TO GABBLE LIKE TINKERS AT THIS TIME OF NIGHT?
SIR TOBY, I MUST BE ROUND WITH YOU. MY LADY BADE ME TELL YOU, THAT, THOUGH SHE HARBOURS YOU AS HER KINSMAN, SHE'S NOTHING ALLIED TO YOUR DISORDERS.
IF YOU CAN SEPARATE YOURSELF AND YOUR MISDEMEANORS, YOU ARE WELCOME TO THE HOUSE; IF NOT, AND IT WOULD PLEASE YOU TO TAKE LEAVE OF HER, SHE IS VERY WILLING TO BID YOU FAREWELL.

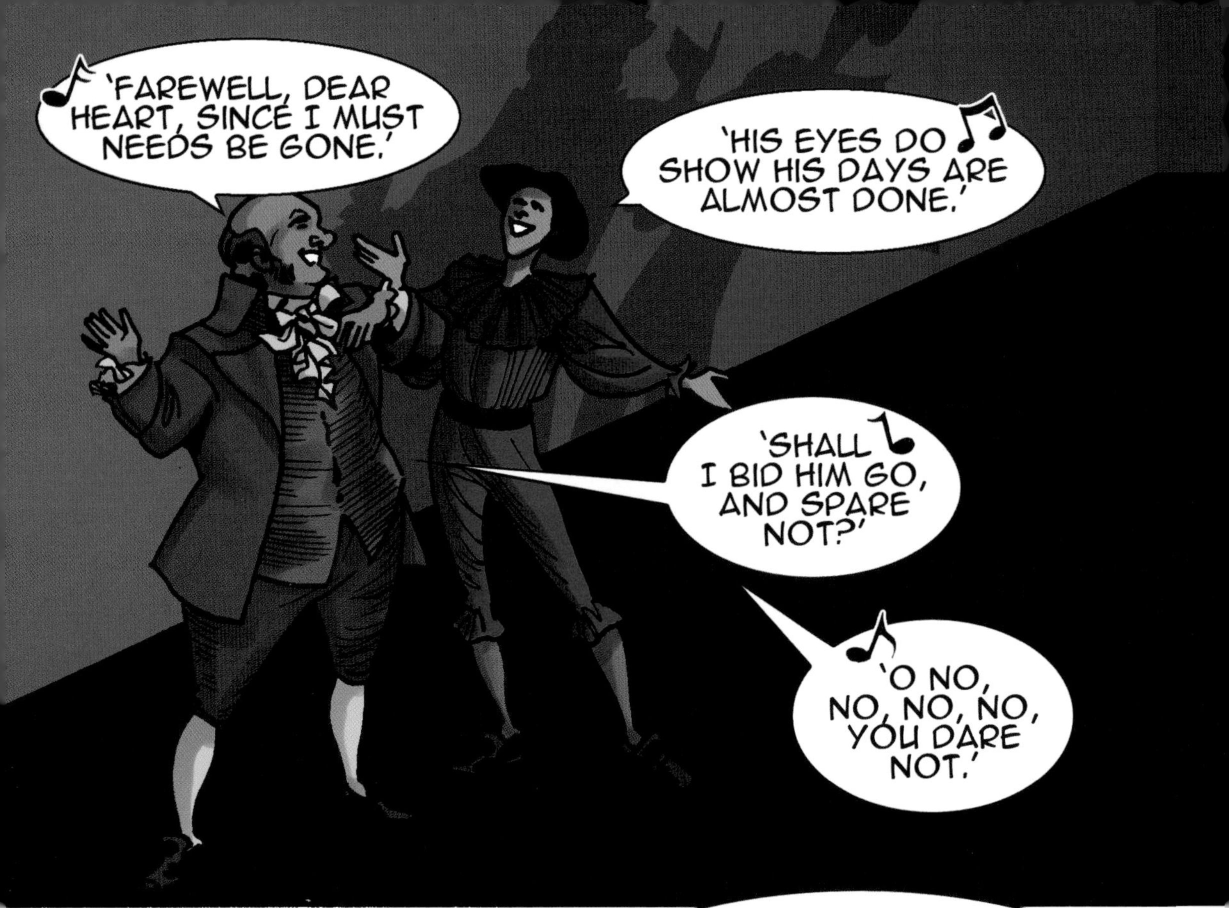
'FAREWELL, DEAR HEART, SINCE I MUST NEEDS BE GONE.'
'HIS EYES DO SHOW HIS DAYS ARE ALMOST DONE.'
'SHALL I BID HIM GO, AND SPARE NOT?'
'O NO, NO, NO, NO, YOU DARE NOT.'

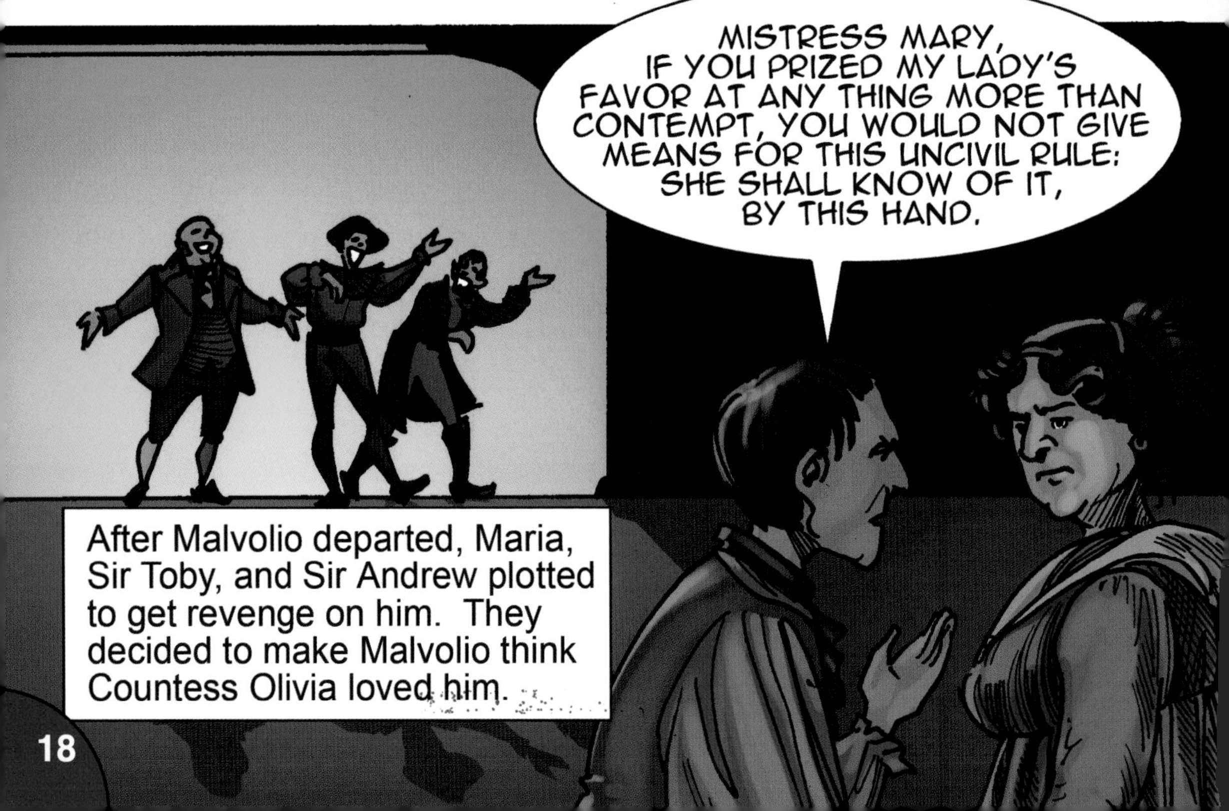
MISTRESS MARY, IF YOU PRIZED MY LADY'S FAVOR AT ANY THING MORE THAN CONTEMPT, YOU WOULD NOT GIVE MEANS FOR THIS UNCIVIL RULE: SHE SHALL KNOW OF IT, BY THIS HAND.

After Malvolio departed, Maria, Sir Toby, and Sir Andrew plotted to get revenge on him. They decided to make Malvolio think Countess Olivia loved him.

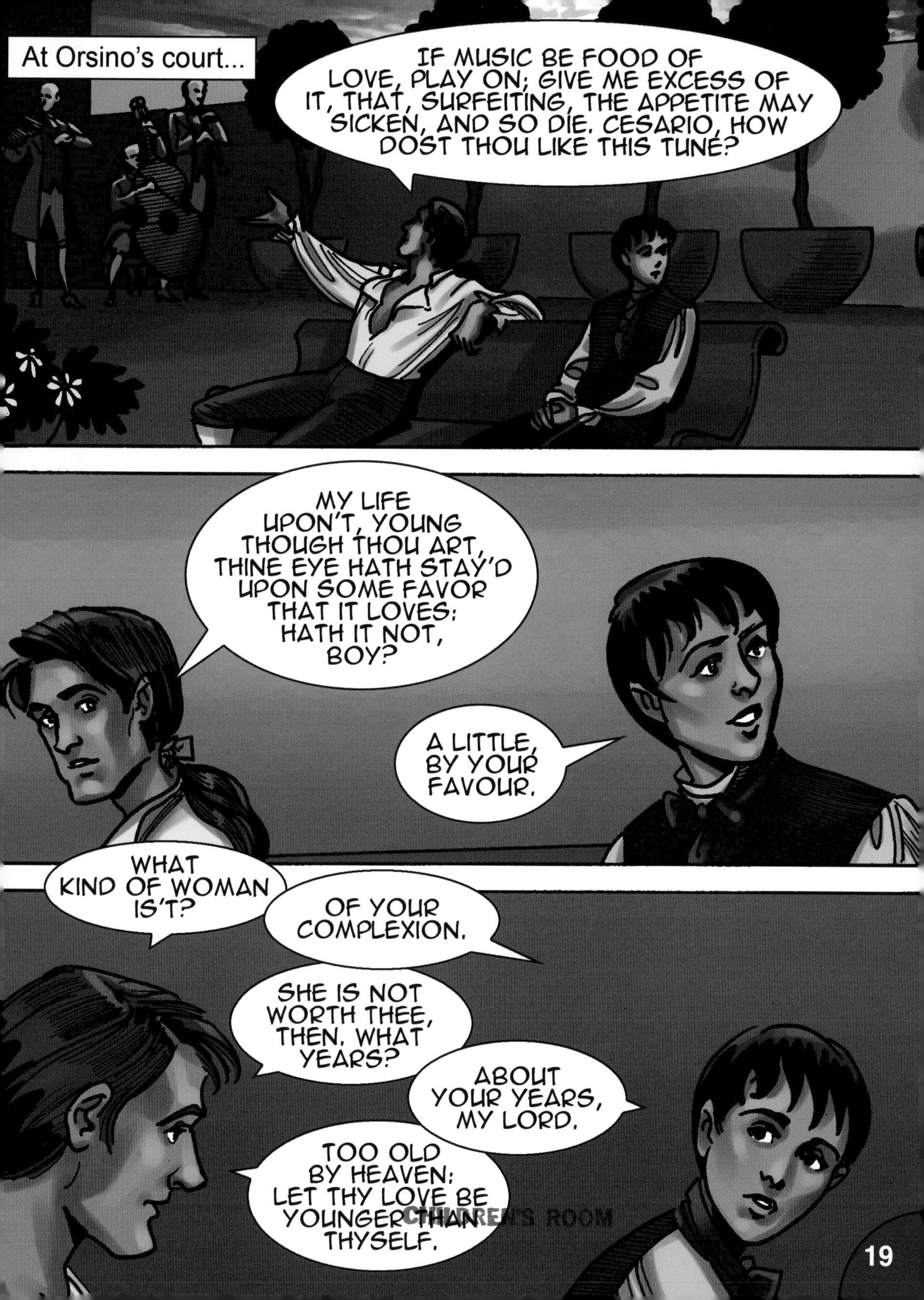
At Orsino's court...
IF MUSIC BE FOOD OF LOVE, PLAY ON; GIVE ME EXCESS OF IT, THAT, SURFEITING, THE APPETITE MAY SICKEN, AND SO DIE. CESARIO, HOW DOST THOU LIKE THIS TUNE?
MY LIFE UPON'T, YOUNG THOUGH THOU ART, THINE EYE HATH STAY'D UPON SOME FAVOR THAT IT LOVES: HATH IT NOT, BOY?
A LITTLE, BY YOUR FAVOUR.
WHAT KIND OF WOMAN IS'T?
OF YOUR COMPLEXION.
SHE IS NOT WORTH THEE, THEN. WHAT YEARS?
ABOUT YOUR YEARS, MY LORD.
TOO OLD BY HEAVEN: LET THY LOVE BE YOUNGER THAN THYSELF.

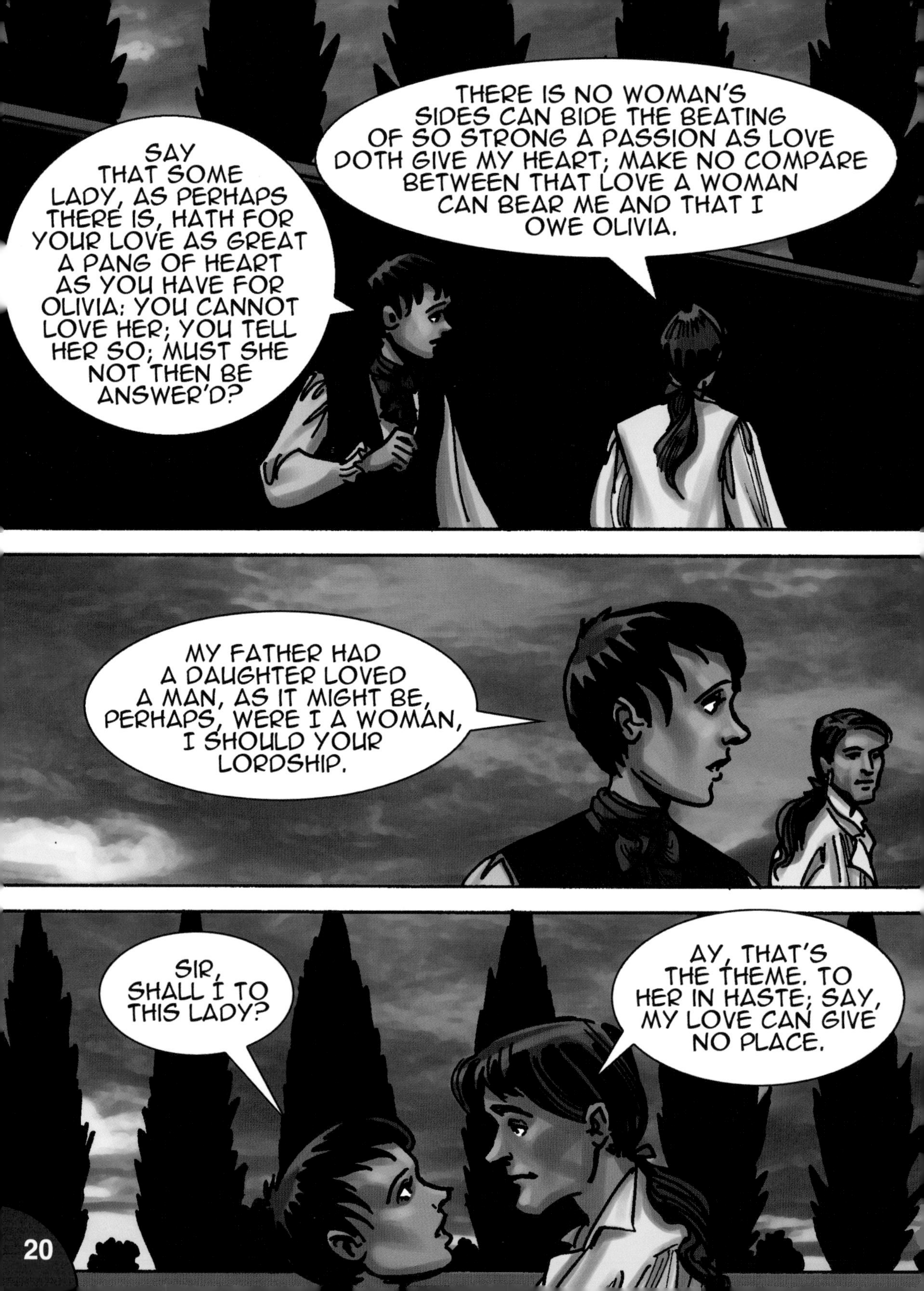
SAY THAT SOME LADY, AS PERHAPS THERE IS, HATH FOR YOUR LOVE AS GREAT A PANG OF HEART AS YOU HAVE FOR OLIVIA: YOU CANNOT LOVE HER; YOU TELL HER SO; MUST SHE NOT THEN BE ANSWER'D?
THERE IS NO WOMAN'S SIDES CAN BIDE THE BEATING OF SO STRONG A PASSION AS LOVE DOTH GIVE MY HEART; MAKE NO COMPARE BETWEEN THAT LOVE A WOMAN CAN BEAR ME AND THAT I OWE OLIVIA.
MY FATHER HAD A DAUGHTER LOVED A MAN, AS IT MIGHT BE, PERHAPS, WERE I A WOMAN, I SHOULD YOUR LORDSHIP.
SIR, SHALL I TO THIS LADY?
AY, THAT'S THE THEME. TO HER IN HASTE; SAY, MY LOVE CAN GIVE NO PLACE.

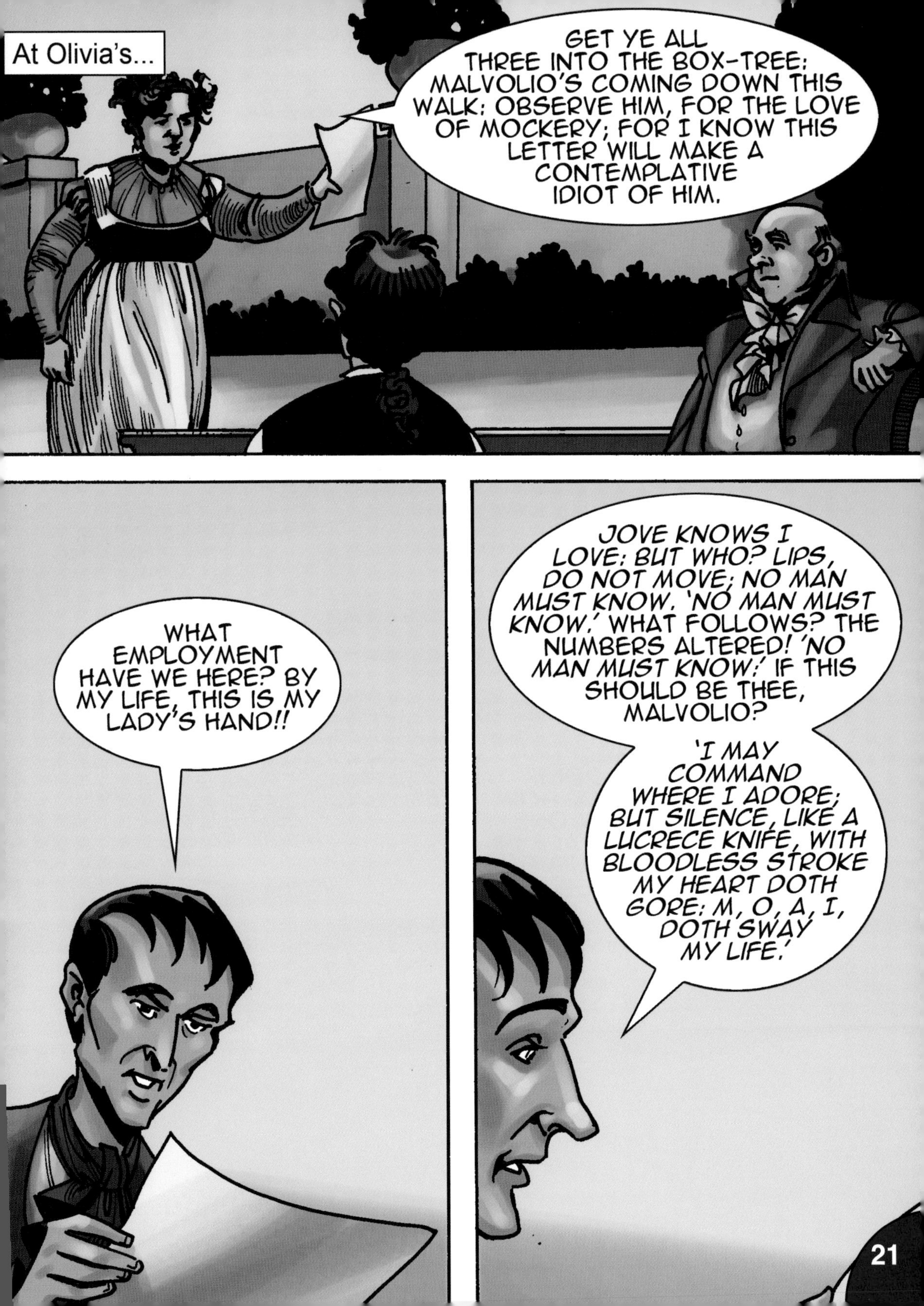
At Olivia's...
GET YE ALL THREE INTO THE BOX-TREE: MALVOLIO'S COMING DOWN THIS WALK: OBSERVE HIM, FOR THE LOVE OF MOCKERY; FOR I KNOW THIS LETTER WILL MAKE A CONTEMPLATIVE IDIOT OF HIM.
WHAT EMPLOYMENT HAVE WE HERE? BY MY LIFE, THIS IS MY LADY'S HAND!!
JOVE KNOWS I LOVE: BUT WHO? LIPS, DO NOT MOVE; NO MAN MUST KNOW. 'NO MAN MUST KNOW.' WHAT FOLLOWS? THE NUMBERS ALTERED! 'NO MAN MUST KNOW:' IF THIS SHOULD BE THEE, MALVOLIO?
'I MAY COMMAND WHERE I ADORE; BUT SILENCE, LIKE A LUCRECE KNIFE, WITH BLOODLESS STROKE MY HEART DOTH GORE: M, O, A, I, DOTH SWAY MY LIFE.'

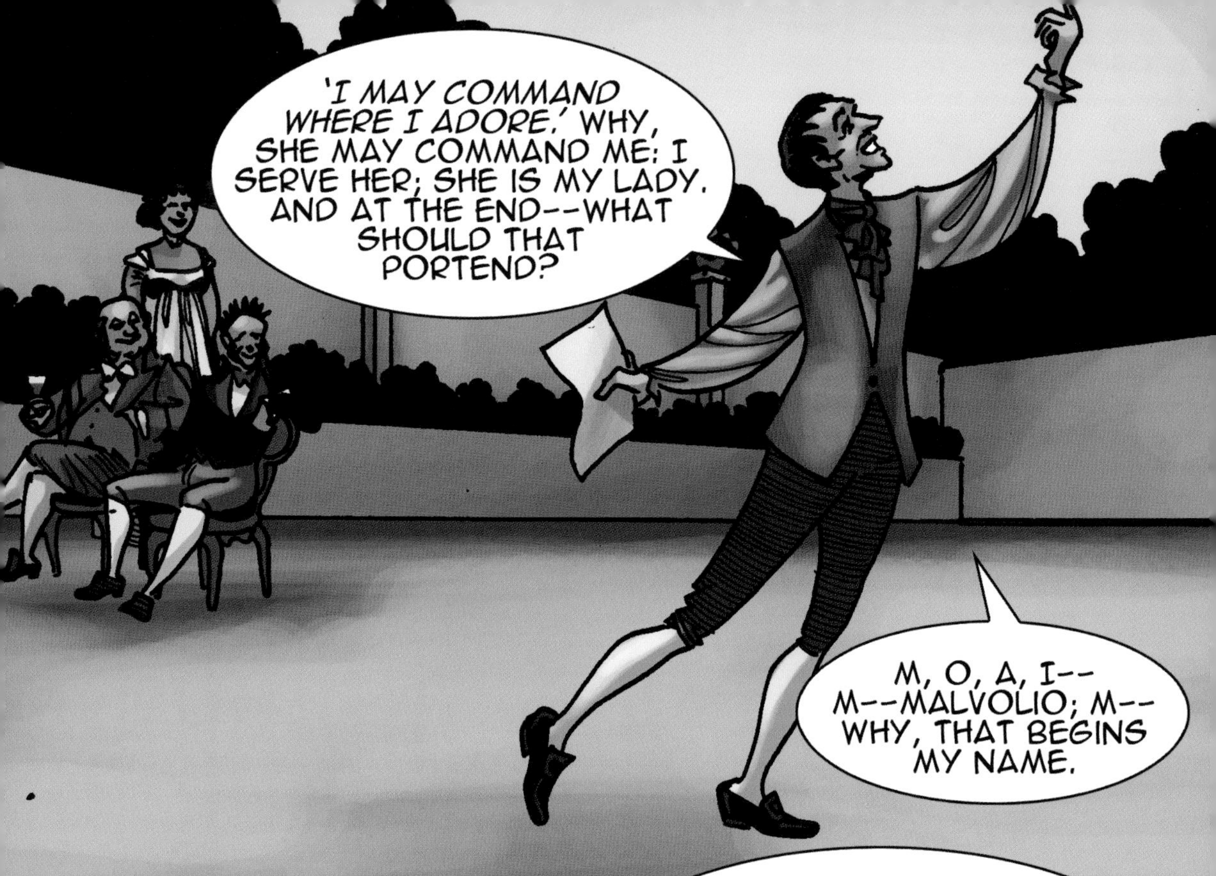
'I MAY COMMAND WHERE I ADORE.' WHY, SHE MAY COMMAND ME: I SERVE HER; SHE IS MY LADY. AND AT THE END--WHAT SHOULD THAT PORTEND?
M, O, A, I-- M--MALVOLIO; M-- WHY, THAT BEGINS MY NAME.

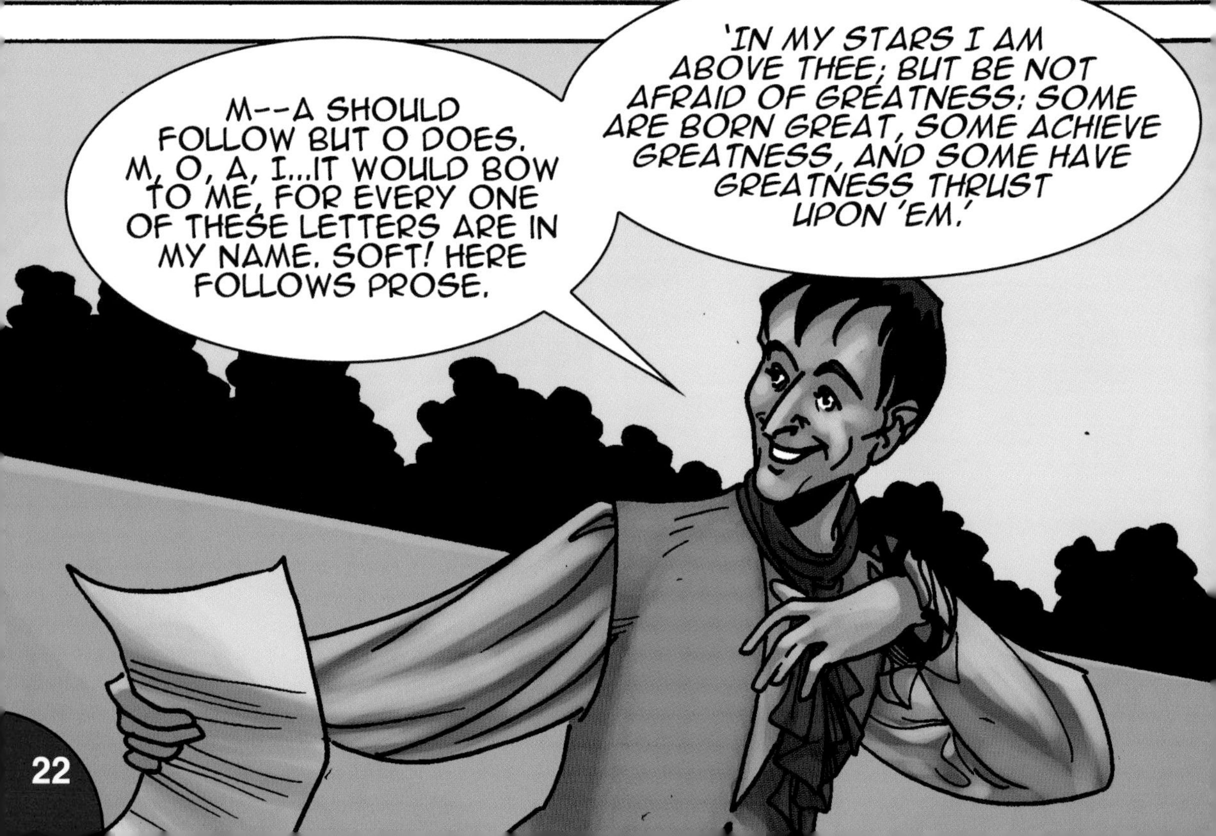
M--A SHOULD FOLLOW BUT O DOES. M, O, A, I...IT WOULD BOW TO ME, FOR EVERY ONE OF THESE LETTERS ARE IN MY NAME. SOFT! HERE FOLLOWS PROSE.
'IN MY STARS I AM ABOVE THEE; BUT BE NOT AFRAID OF GREATNESS: SOME ARE BORN GREAT, SOME ACHIEVE GREATNESS, AND SOME HAVE GREATNESS THRUST UPON 'EM.'

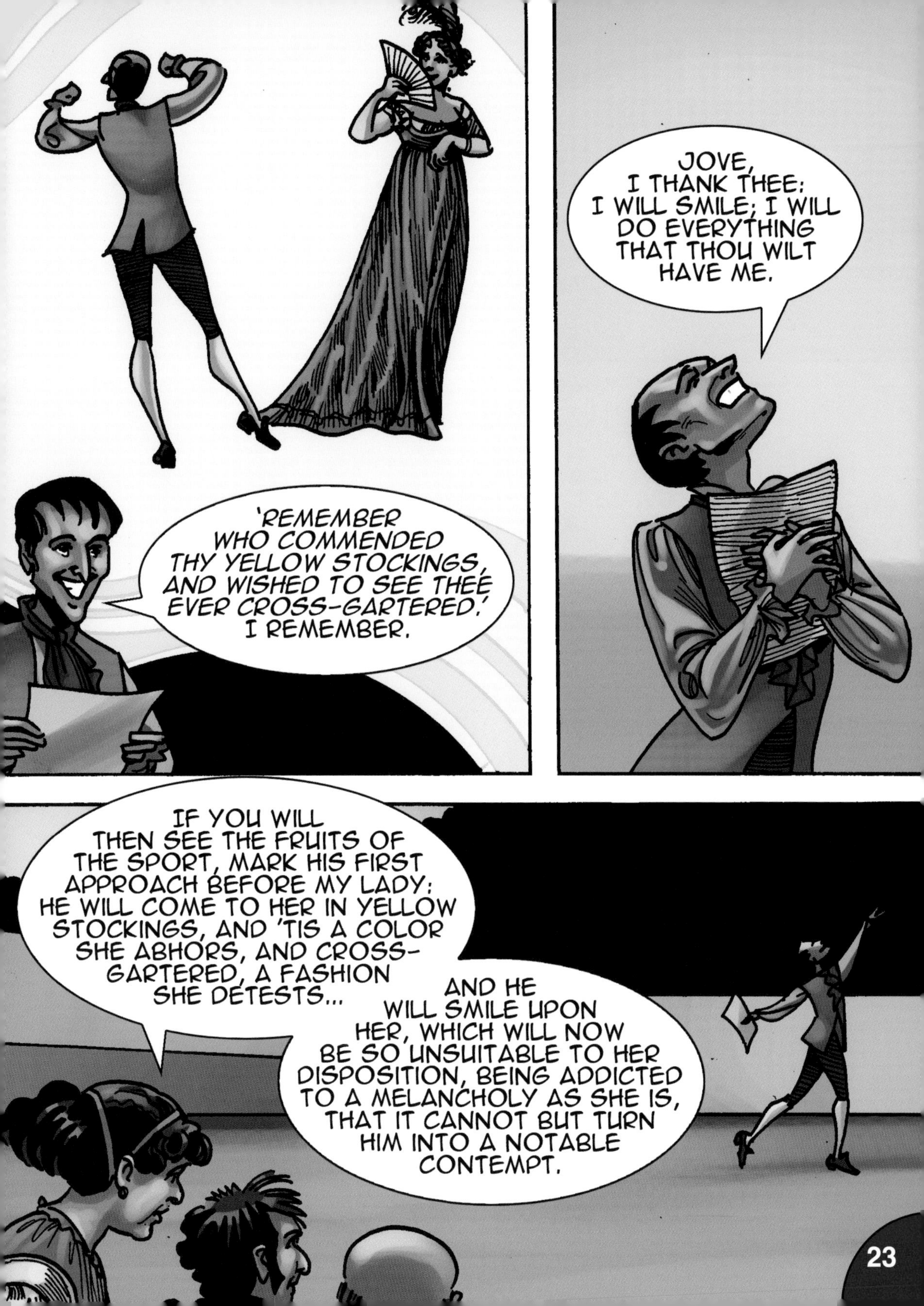
JOVE, I THANK THEE: I WILL SMILE; I WILL DO EVERYTHING THAT THOU WILT HAVE ME.
'REMEMBER WHO COMMENDED THY YELLOW STOCKINGS, AND WISHED TO SEE THEE EVER CROSS-GARTERED.' I REMEMBER.
IF YOU WILL THEN SEE THE FRUITS OF THE SPORT, MARK HIS FIRST APPROACH BEFORE MY LADY: HE WILL COME TO HER IN YELLOW STOCKINGS, AND 'TIS A COLOR SHE ABHORS, AND CROSS-GARTERED, A FASHION SHE DETESTS...
AND HE WILL SMILE UPON HER, WHICH WILL NOW BE SO UNSUITABLE TO HER DISPOSITION, BEING ADDICTED TO A MELANCHOLY AS SHE IS, THAT IT CANNOT BUT TURN HIM INTO A NOTABLE CONTEMPT.

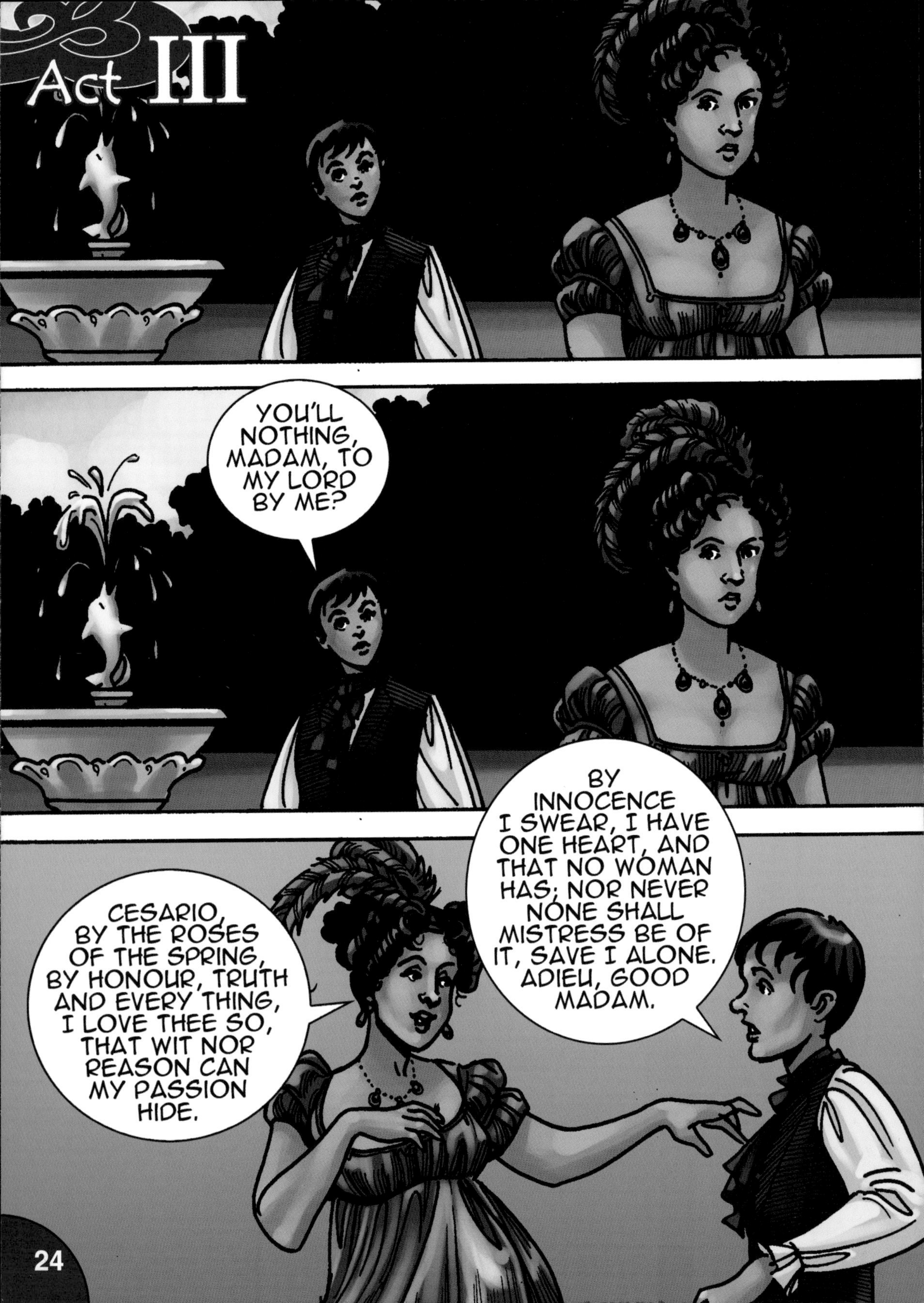
Act III
YOU'LL NOTHING, MADAM, TO MY LORD BY ME?
CESARIO, BY THE ROSES OF THE SPRING, BY HONOUR, TRUTH AND EVERY THING, I LOVE THEE SO, THAT WIT NOR REASON CAN MY PASSION HIDE.
BY INNOCENCE I SWEAR, I HAVE ONE HEART, AND THAT NO WOMAN HAS; NOR NEVER NONE SHALL MISTRESS BE OF IT, SAVE I ALONE. ADIEU, GOOD MADAM.

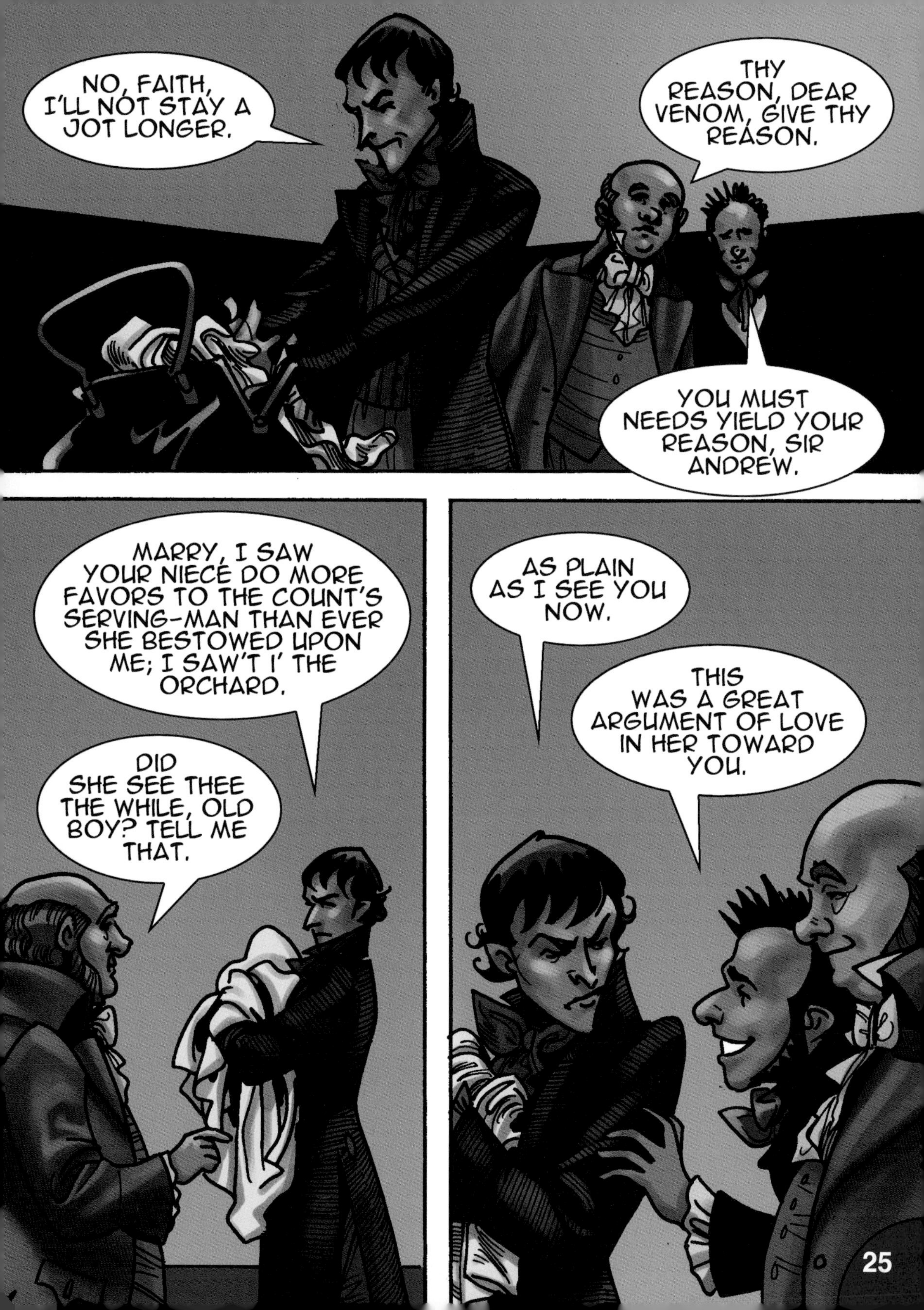
NO, FAITH, I'LL NOT STAY A JOT LONGER.
THY REASON, DEAR VENOM, GIVE THY REASON.
YOU MUST NEEDS YIELD YOUR REASON, SIR ANDREW.
MARRY, I SAW YOUR NIECE DO MORE FAVORS TO THE COUNT'S SERVING-MAN THAN EVER SHE BESTOWED UPON ME; I SAW'T I' THE ORCHARD.
DID SHE SEE THEE THE WHILE, OLD BOY? TELL ME THAT.
AS PLAIN AS I SEE YOU NOW.
THIS WAS A GREAT ARGUMENT OF LOVE IN HER TOWARD YOU.

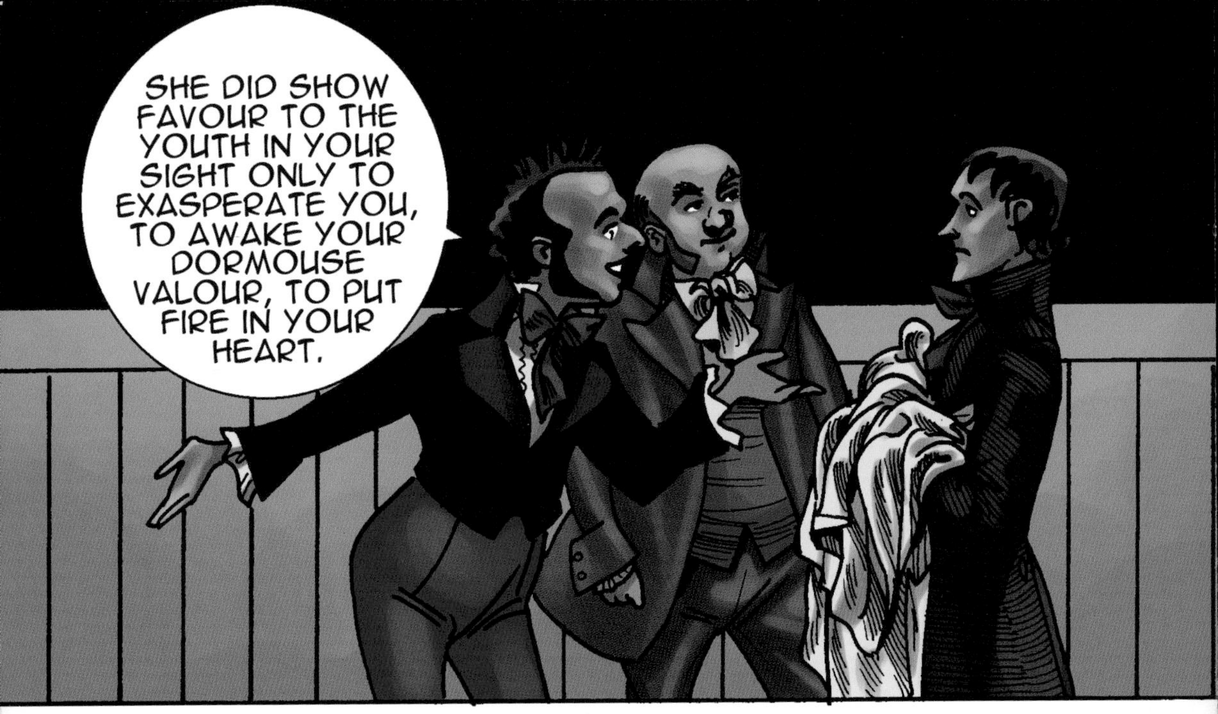
SHE DID SHOW FAVOUR TO THE YOUTH IN YOUR SIGHT ONLY TO EXASPERATE YOU, TO AWAKE YOUR DORMOUSE VALOUR, TO PUT FIRE IN YOUR HEART.

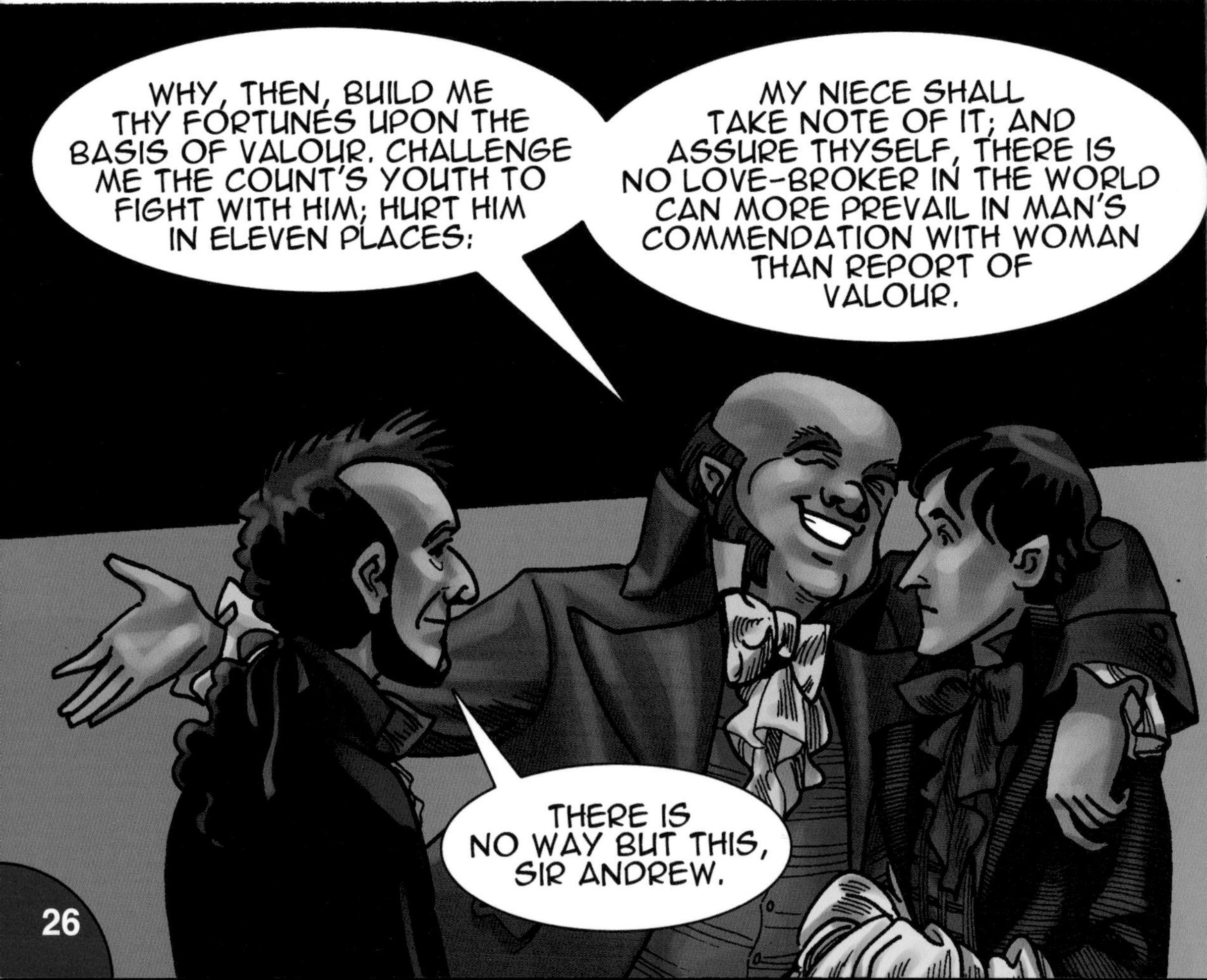
WHY, THEN, BUILD ME THY FORTUNES UPON THE BASIS OF VALOUR. CHALLENGE ME THE COUNT'S YOUTH TO FIGHT WITH HIM; HURT HIM IN ELEVEN PLACES:
MY NIECE SHALL TAKE NOTE OF IT; AND ASSURE THYSELF, THERE IS NO LOVE-BROKER IN THE WORLD CAN MORE PREVAIL IN MAN'S COMMENDATION WITH WOMAN THAN REPORT OF VALOUR.
THERE IS NO WAY BUT THIS, SIR ANDREW.

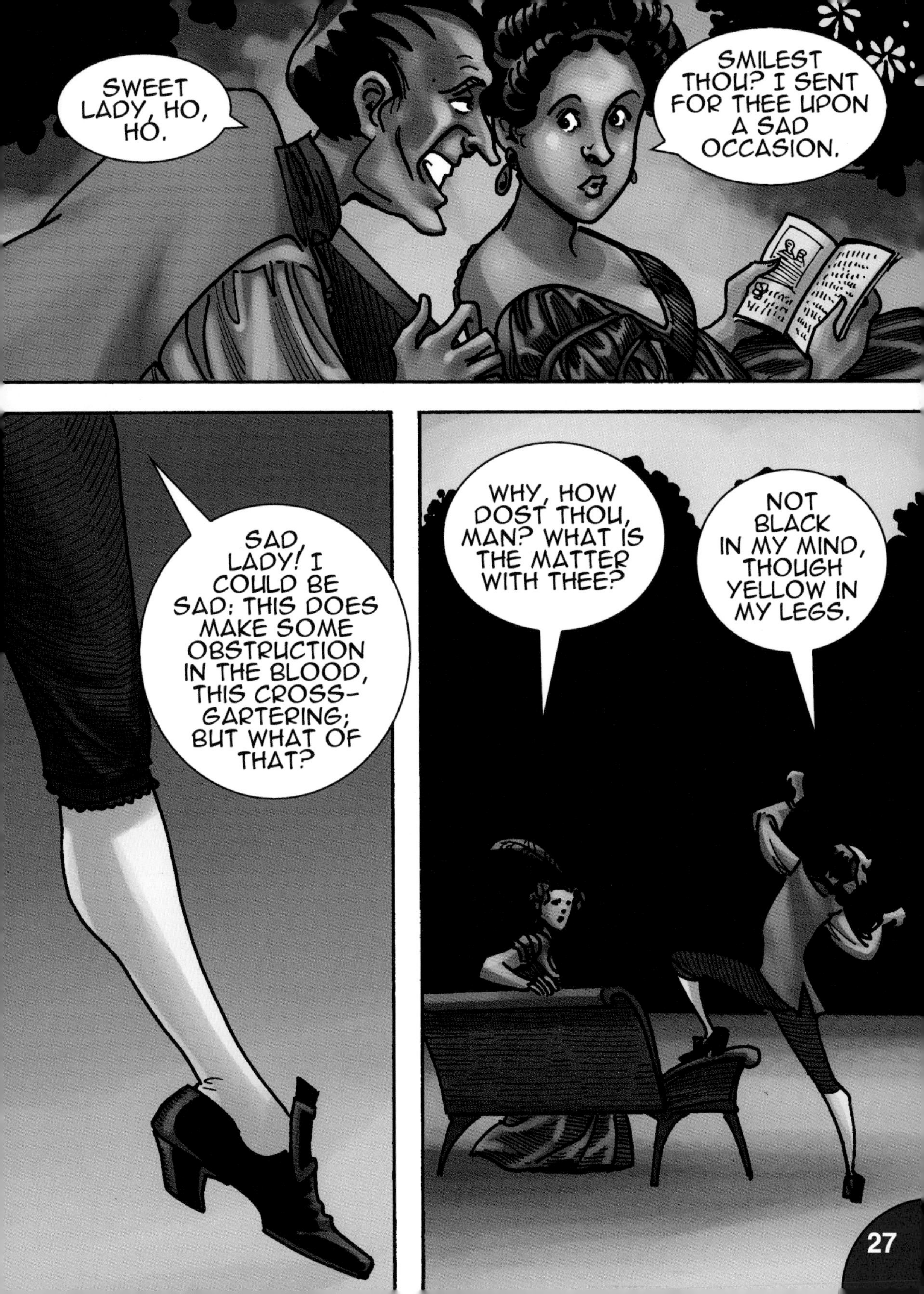
SWEET LADY, HO, HO.
SMILEST THOU? I SENT FOR THEE UPON A SAD OCCASION.
SAD, LADY! I COULD BE SAD: THIS DOES MAKE SOME OBSTRUCTION IN THE BLOOD, THIS CROSS-GARTERING; BUT WHAT OF THAT?
WHY, HOW DOST THOU, MAN? WHAT IS THE MATTER WITH THEE?
NOT BLACK IN MY MIND, THOUGH YELLOW IN MY LEGS.

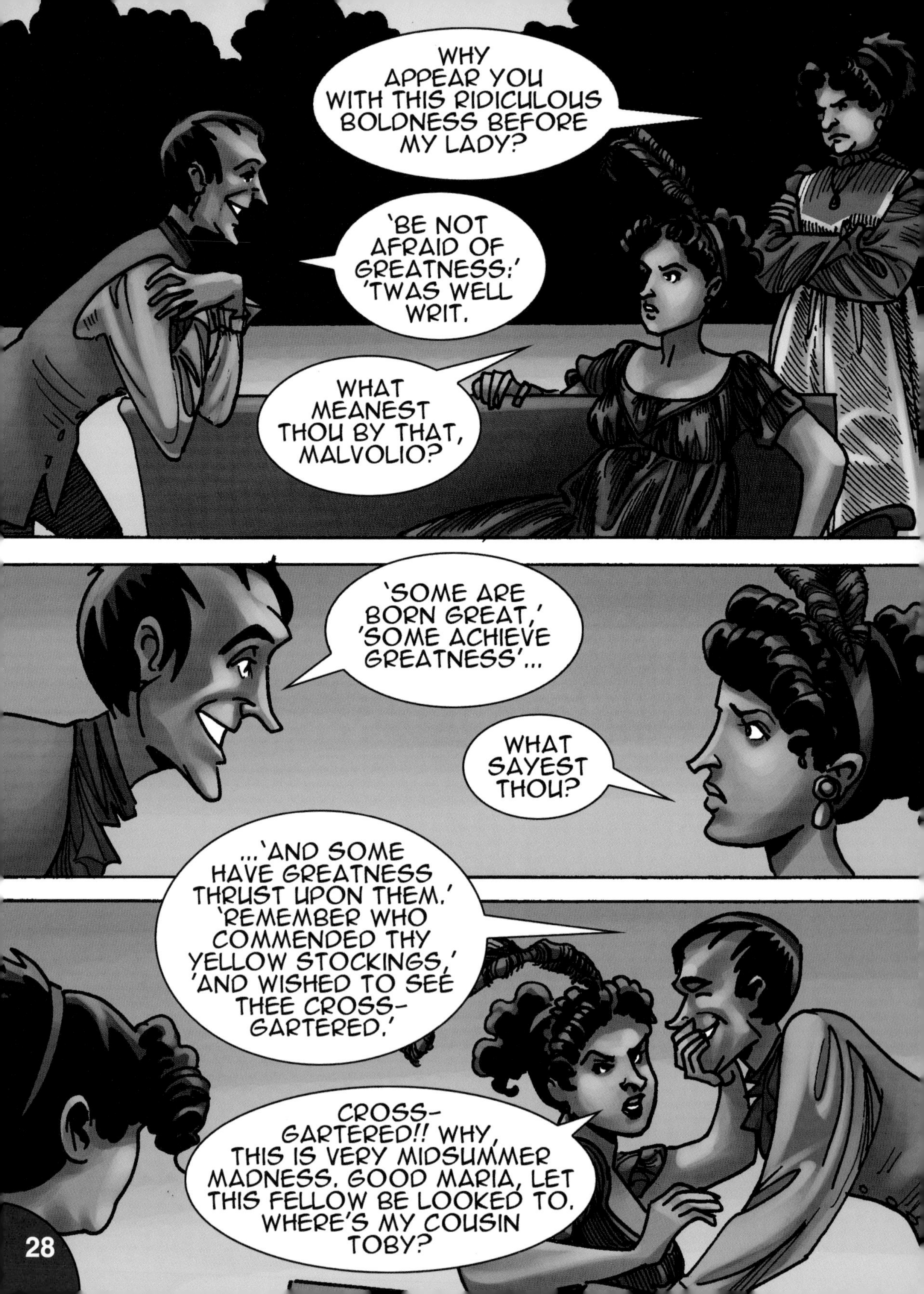
WHY APPEAR YOU WITH THIS RIDICULOUS BOLDNESS BEFORE MY LADY?
'BE NOT AFRAID OF GREATNESS:' 'TWAS WELL WRIT.
WHAT MEANEST THOU BY THAT, MALVOLIO?
'SOME ARE BORN GREAT,' 'SOME ACHIEVE GREATNESS'...
WHAT SAYEST THOU?
...'AND SOME HAVE GREATNESS THRUST UPON THEM.' 'REMEMBER WHO COMMENDED THY YELLOW STOCKINGS,' 'AND WISHED TO SEE THEE CROSS-GARTERED.'
CROSS-GARTERED!! WHY, THIS IS VERY MIDSUMMER MADNESS. GOOD MARIA, LET THIS FELLOW BE LOOKED TO. WHERE'S MY COUSIN TOBY?

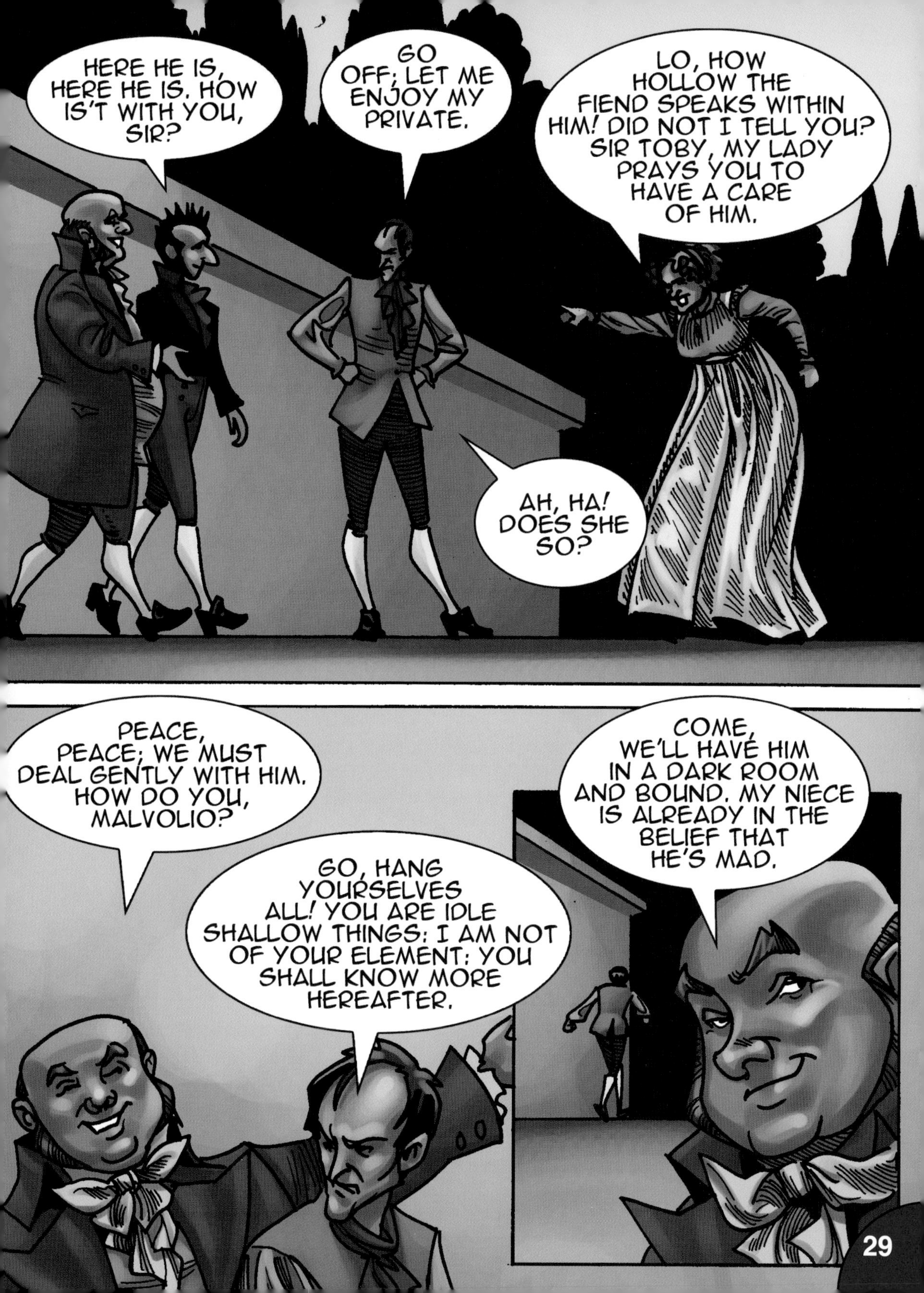
HERE HE IS, HERE HE IS. HOW IS'T WITH YOU, SIR?
GO OFF; LET ME ENJOY MY PRIVATE.
LO, HOW HOLLOW THE FIEND SPEAKS WITHIN HIM! DID NOT I TELL YOU? SIR TOBY, MY LADY PRAYS YOU TO HAVE A CARE OF HIM.
AH, HA! DOES SHE SO?
PEACE, PEACE; WE MUST DEAL GENTLY WITH HIM. HOW DO YOU, MALVOLIO?
GO, HANG YOURSELVES ALL! YOU ARE IDLE SHALLOW THINGS: I AM NOT OF YOUR ELEMENT: YOU SHALL KNOW MORE HEREAFTER.
COME, WE'LL HAVE HIM IN A DARK ROOM AND BOUND. MY NIECE IS ALREADY IN THE BELIEF THAT HE'S MAD.

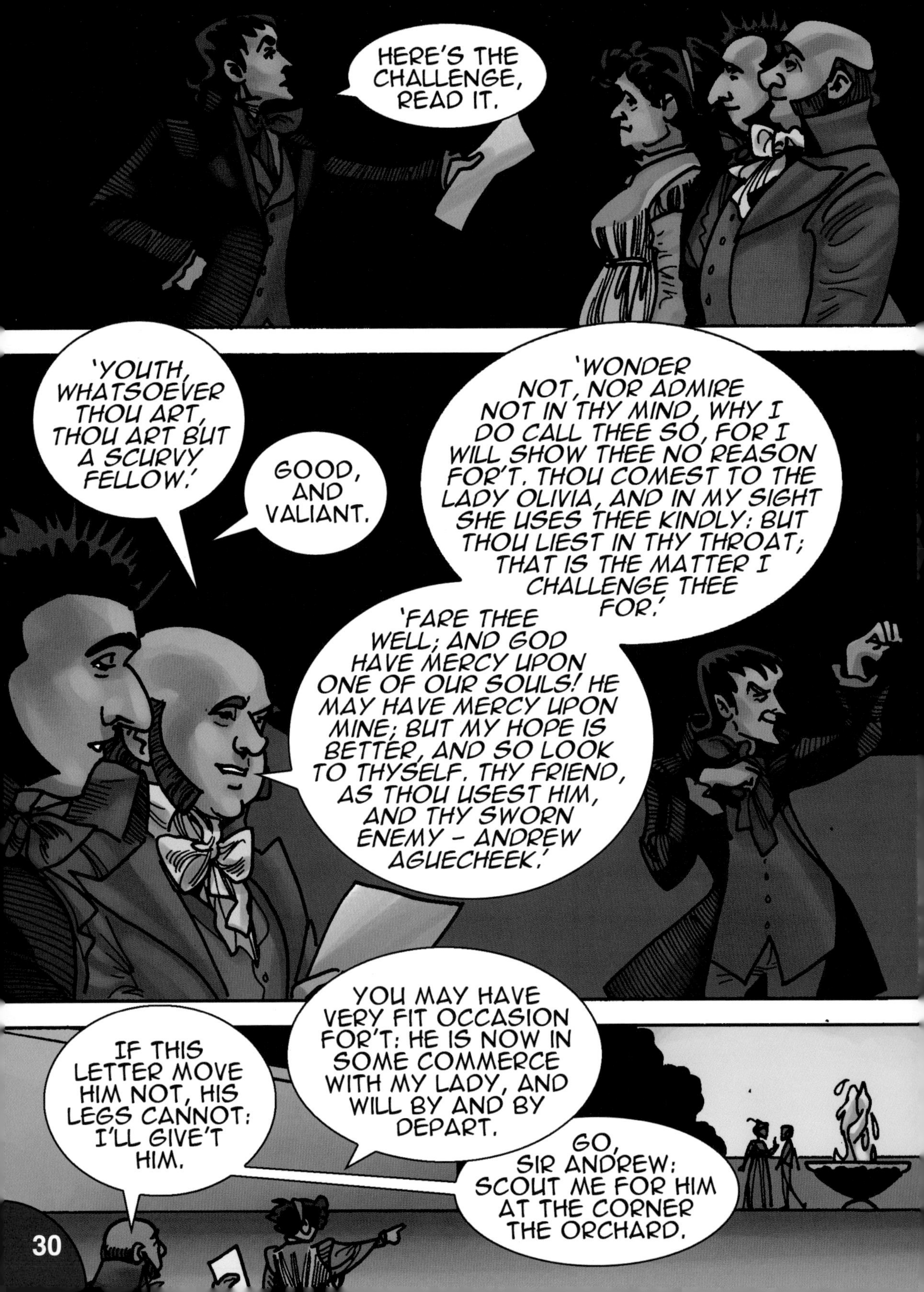
HERE'S THE CHALLENGE, READ IT.
'YOUTH, WHATSOEVER THOU ART, THOU ART BUT A SCURVY FELLOW.'
GOOD, AND VALIANT.
'WONDER NOT, NOR ADMIRE NOT IN THY MIND, WHY I DO CALL THEE SO, FOR I WILL SHOW THEE NO REASON FOR'T. THOU COMEST TO THE LADY OLIVIA, AND IN MY SIGHT SHE USES THEE KINDLY: BUT THOU LIEST IN THY THROAT; THAT IS THE MATTER I CHALLENGE THEE FOR.'
'FARE THEE WELL; AND GOD HAVE MERCY UPON ONE OF OUR SOULS! HE MAY HAVE MERCY UPON MINE; BUT MY HOPE IS BETTER, AND SO LOOK TO THYSELF. THY FRIEND, AS THOU USEST HIM, AND THY SWORN ENEMY - ANDREW AGUECHEEK.'
IF THIS LETTER MOVE HIM NOT, HIS LEGS CANNOT: I'LL GIVE'T HIM.
YOU MAY HAVE VERY FIT OCCASION FOR'T: HE IS NOW IN SOME COMMERCE WITH MY LADY, AND WILL BY AND BY DEPART.
GO, SIR ANDREW: SCOUT ME FOR HIM AT THE CORNER THE ORCHARD.

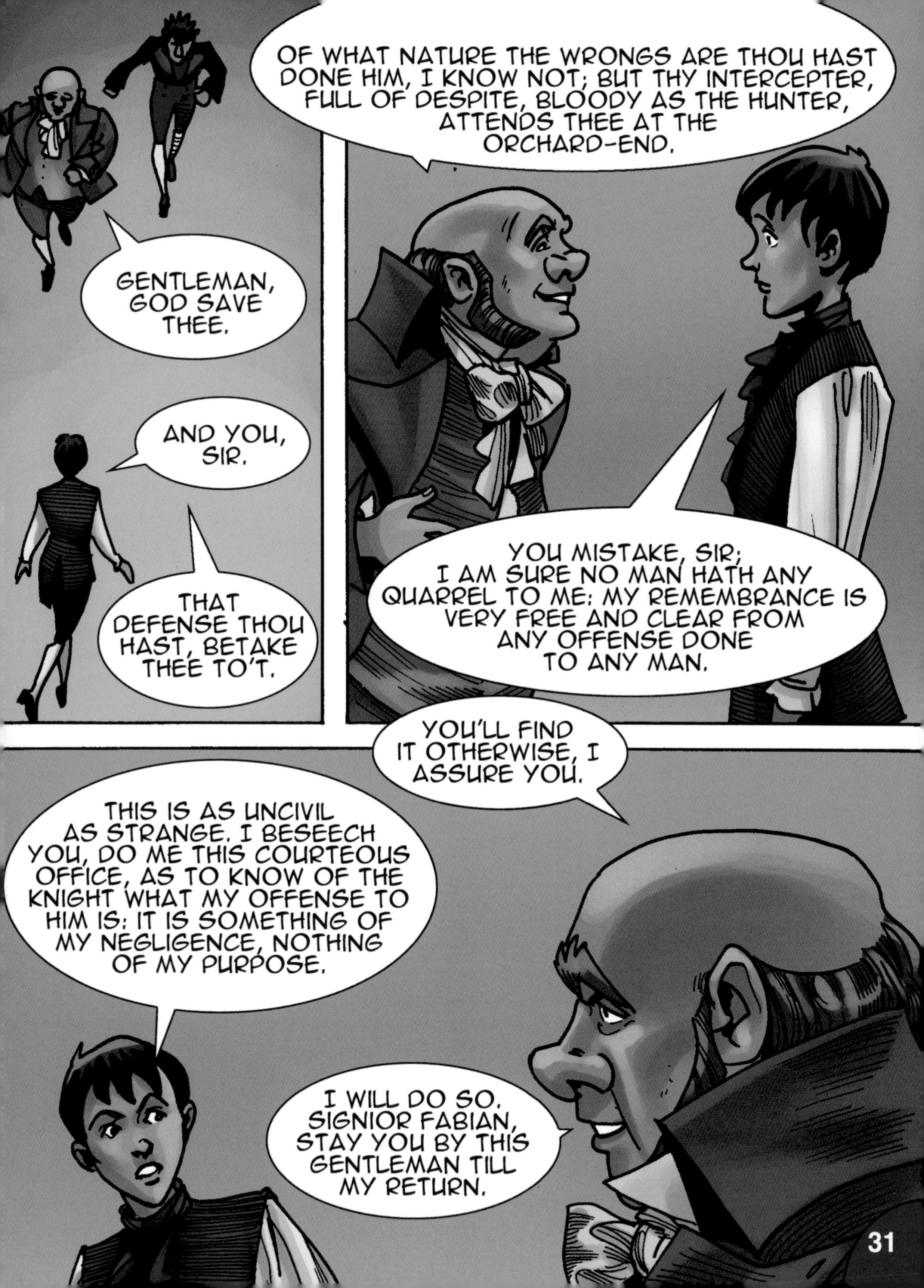
GENTLEMAN, GOD SAVE THEE.
AND YOU, SIR.
THAT DEFENSE THOU HAST, BETAKE THEE TO'T.
OF WHAT NATURE THE WRONGS ARE THOU HAST DONE HIM, I KNOW NOT; BUT THY INTERCEPTER, FULL OF DESPITE, BLOODY AS THE HUNTER, ATTENDS THEE AT THE ORCHARD-END.
YOU MISTAKE, SIR; I AM SURE NO MAN HATH ANY QUARREL TO ME: MY REMEMBRANCE IS VERY FREE AND CLEAR FROM ANY OFFENSE DONE TO ANY MAN.
YOU'LL FIND IT OTHERWISE, I ASSURE YOU.
THIS IS AS UNCIVIL AS STRANGE. I BESEECH YOU, DO ME THIS COURTEOUS OFFICE, AS TO KNOW OF THE KNIGHT WHAT MY OFFENSE TO HIM IS: IT IS SOMETHING OF MY NEGLIGENCE, NOTHING OF MY PURPOSE.
I WILL DO SO. SIGNIOR FABIAN, STAY YOU BY THIS GENTLEMAN TILL MY RETURN.

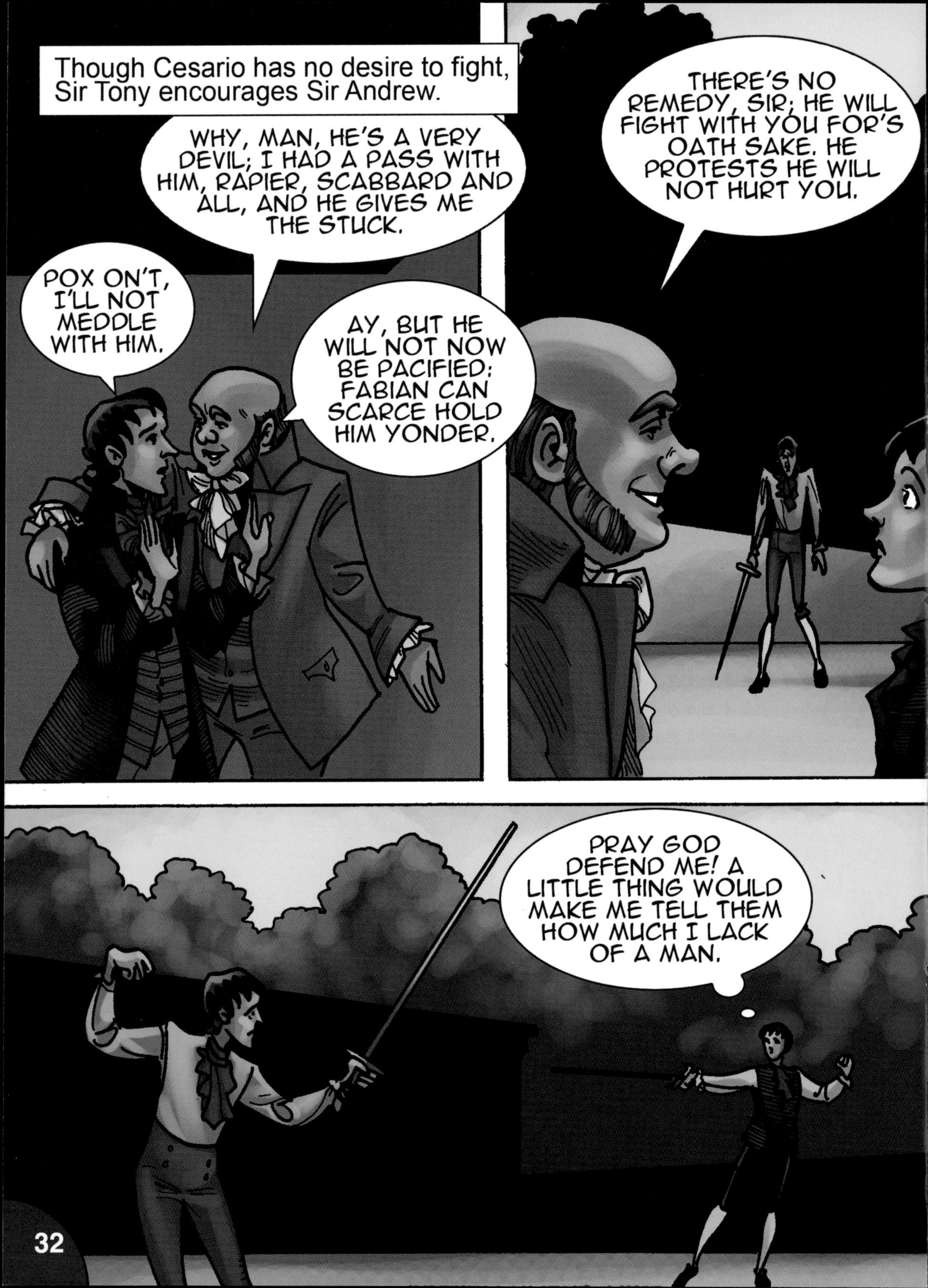
Though Cesario has no desire to fight, Sir Tony encourages Sir Andrew.
WHY, MAN, HE'S A VERY DEVIL; I HAD A PASS WITH HIM, RAPIER, SCABBARD AND ALL, AND HE GIVES ME THE STUCK.
POX ON'T, I'LL NOT MEDDLE WITH HIM.
AY, BUT HE WILL NOT NOW BE PACIFIED: FABIAN CAN SCARCE HOLD HIM YONDER.
THERE'S NO REMEDY, SIR; HE WILL FIGHT WITH YOU FOR'S OATH SAKE. HE PROTESTS HE WILL NOT HURT YOU.
PRAY GOD DEFEND ME! A LITTLE THING WOULD MAKE ME TELL THEM HOW MUCH I LACK OF A MAN.

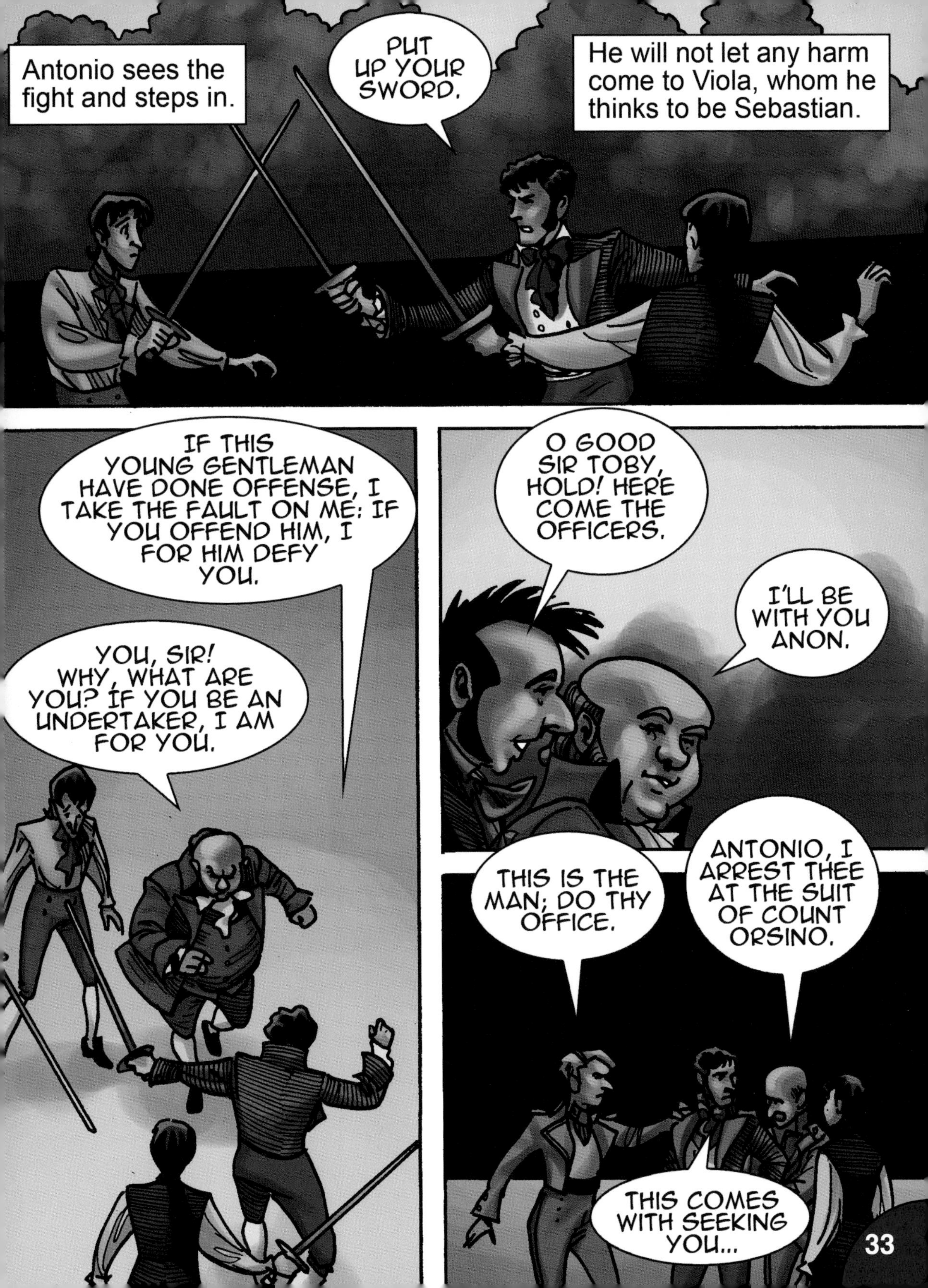

Antonio sees the fight and steps in.
PUT UP YOUR SWORD.
He will not let any harm come to Viola, whom he thinks to be Sebastian.
IF THIS YOUNG GENTLEMAN HAVE DONE OFFENSE, I TAKE THE FAULT ON ME: IF YOU OFFEND HIM, I FOR HIM DEFY YOU.
YOU, SIR! WHY, WHAT ARE YOU? IF YOU BE AN UNDERTAKER, I AM FOR YOU.
O GOOD SIR TOBY, HOLD! HERE COME THE OFFICERS.
I'LL BE WITH YOU ANON.
THIS IS THE MAN; DO THY OFFICE.
ANTONIO, I ARREST THEE AT THE SUIT OF COUNT ORSINO.
THIS COMES WITH SEEKING YOU...

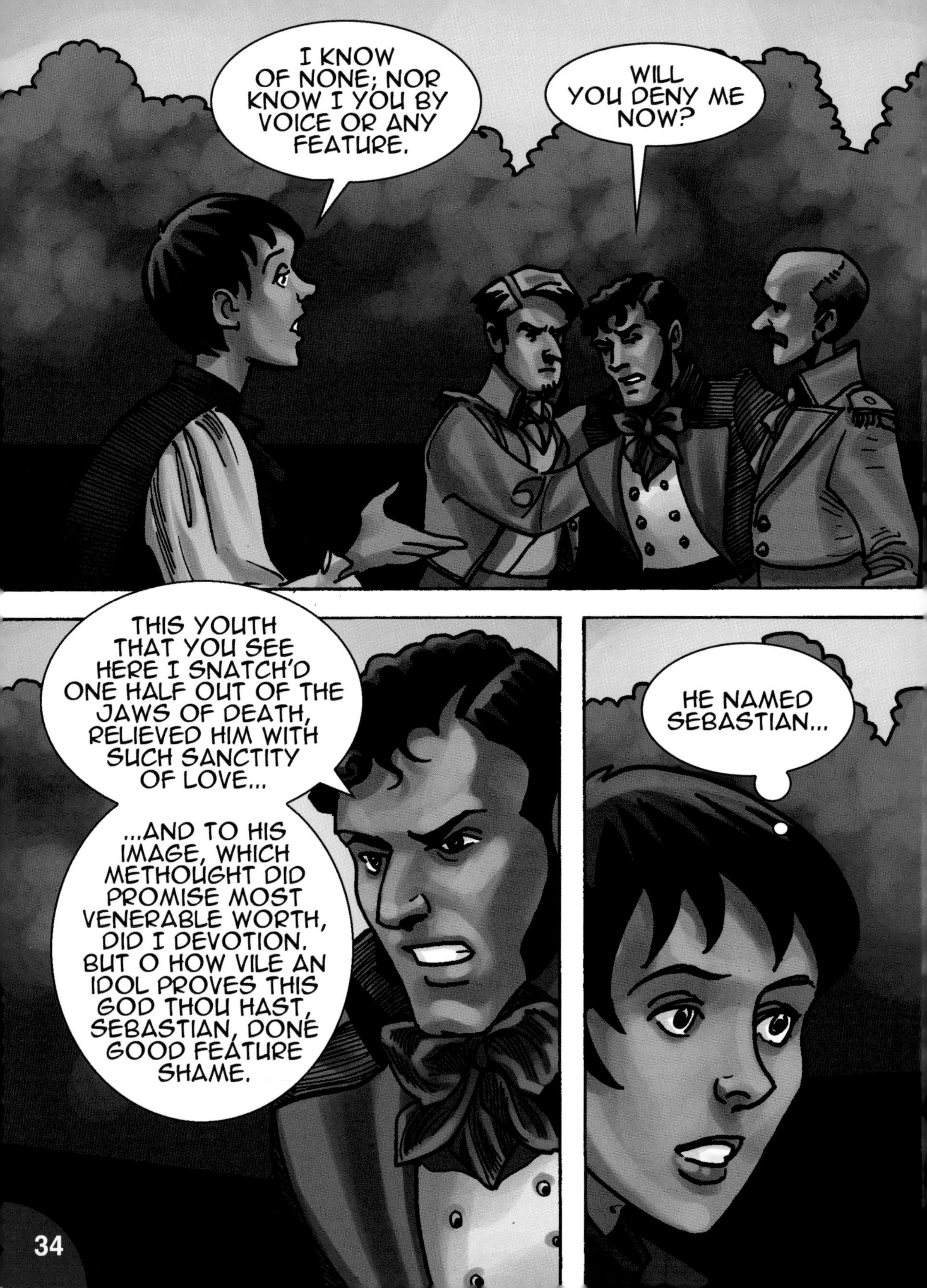
I KNOW OF NONE; NOR KNOW I YOU BY VOICE OR ANY FEATURE.
WILL YOU DENY ME NOW?
THIS YOUTH THAT YOU SEE HERE I SNATCH'D ONE HALF OUT OF THE JAWS OF DEATH, RELIEVED HIM WITH SUCH SANCTITY OF LOVE...
...AND TO HIS IMAGE, WHICH METHOUGHT DID PROMISE MOST VENERABLE WORTH, DID I DEVOTION. BUT O HOW VILE AN IDOL PROVES THIS GOD THOU HAST, SEBASTIAN, DONE GOOD FEATURE SHAME.
HE NAMED SEBASTIAN...

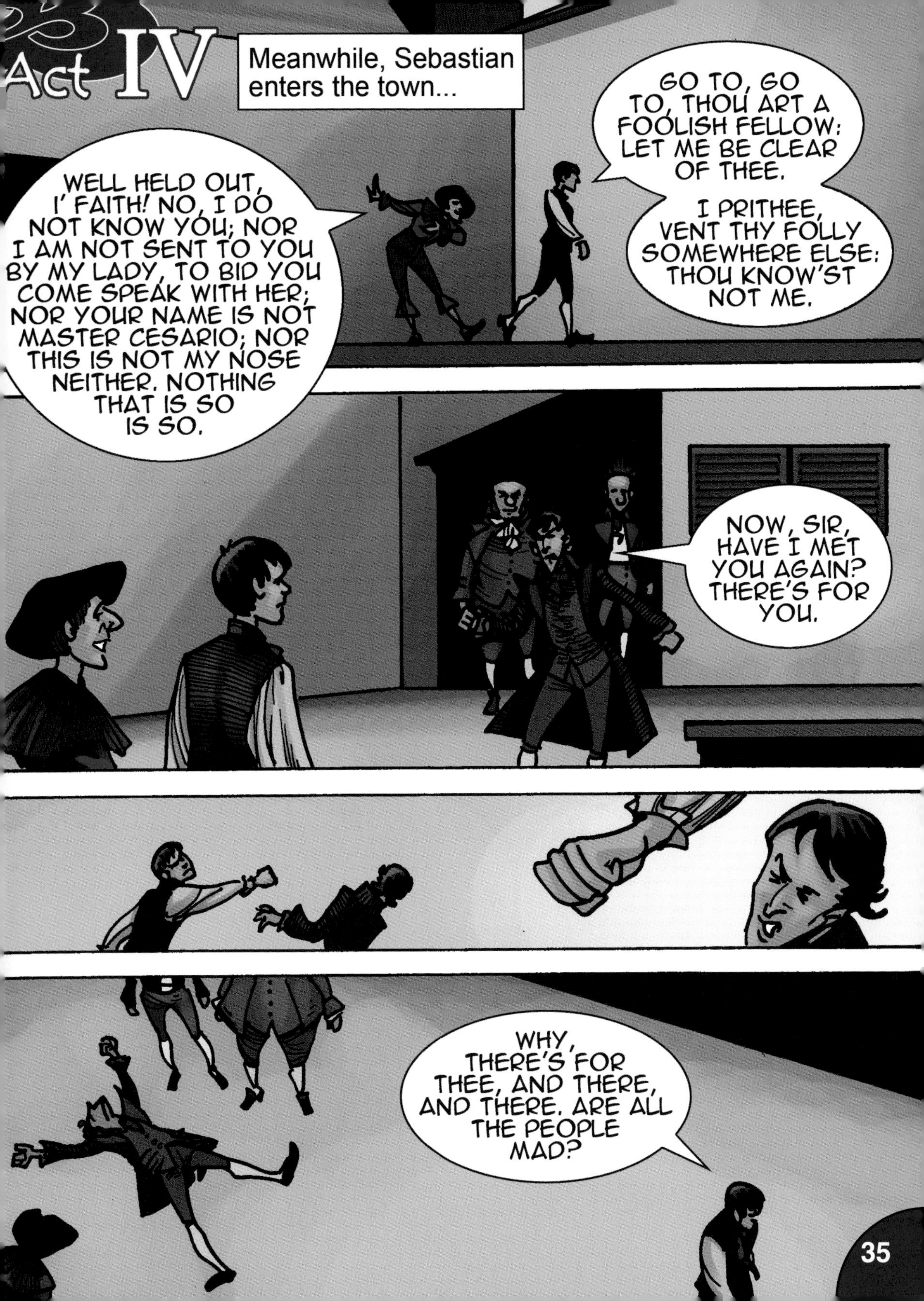
Act IV
Meanwhile, Sebastian enters the town...
WELL HELD OUT, I' FAITH! NO, I DO NOT KNOW YOU; NOR I AM NOT SENT TO YOU BY MY LADY, TO BID YOU COME SPEAK WITH HER; NOR YOUR NAME IS NOT MASTER CESARIO; NOR THIS IS NOT MY NOSE NEITHER. NOTHING THAT IS SO IS SO.
GO TO, GO TO, THOU ART A FOOLISH FELLOW: LET ME BE CLEAR OF THEE.
I PRITHEE, VENT THY FOLLY SOMEWHERE ELSE: THOU KNOW'ST NOT ME.
NOW, SIR, HAVE I MET YOU AGAIN? THERE'S FOR YOU.
WHY, THERE'S FOR THEE, AND THERE, AND THERE. ARE ALL THE PEOPLE MAD?

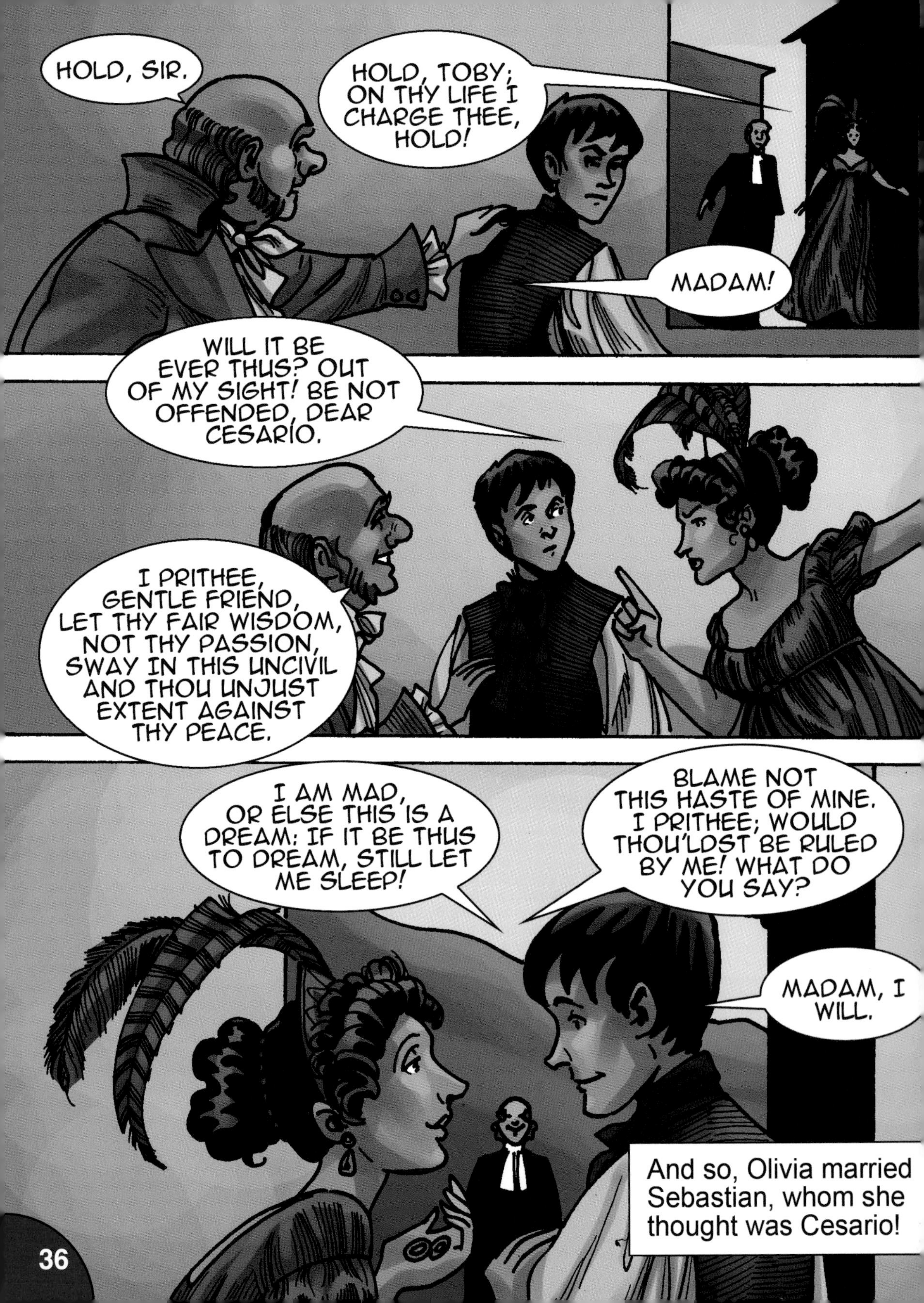
HOLD, SIR.
HOLD, TOBY; ON THY LIFE I CHARGE THEE, HOLD!
MADAM!
WILL IT BE EVER THUS? OUT OF MY SIGHT! BE NOT OFFENDED, DEAR CESARIO.
I PRITHEE, GENTLE FRIEND, LET THY FAIR WISDOM, NOT THY PASSION, SWAY IN THIS UNCIVIL AND THOU UNJUST EXTENT AGAINST THY PEACE.
I AM MAD, OR ELSE THIS IS A DREAM: IF IT BE THUS TO DREAM, STILL LET ME SLEEP!
BLAME NOT THIS HASTE OF MINE. I PRITHEE; WOULD THOU'LDST BE RULED BY ME! WHAT DO YOU SAY?
MADAM, I WILL.
And so, Olivia married Sebastian, whom she thought was Cesario!

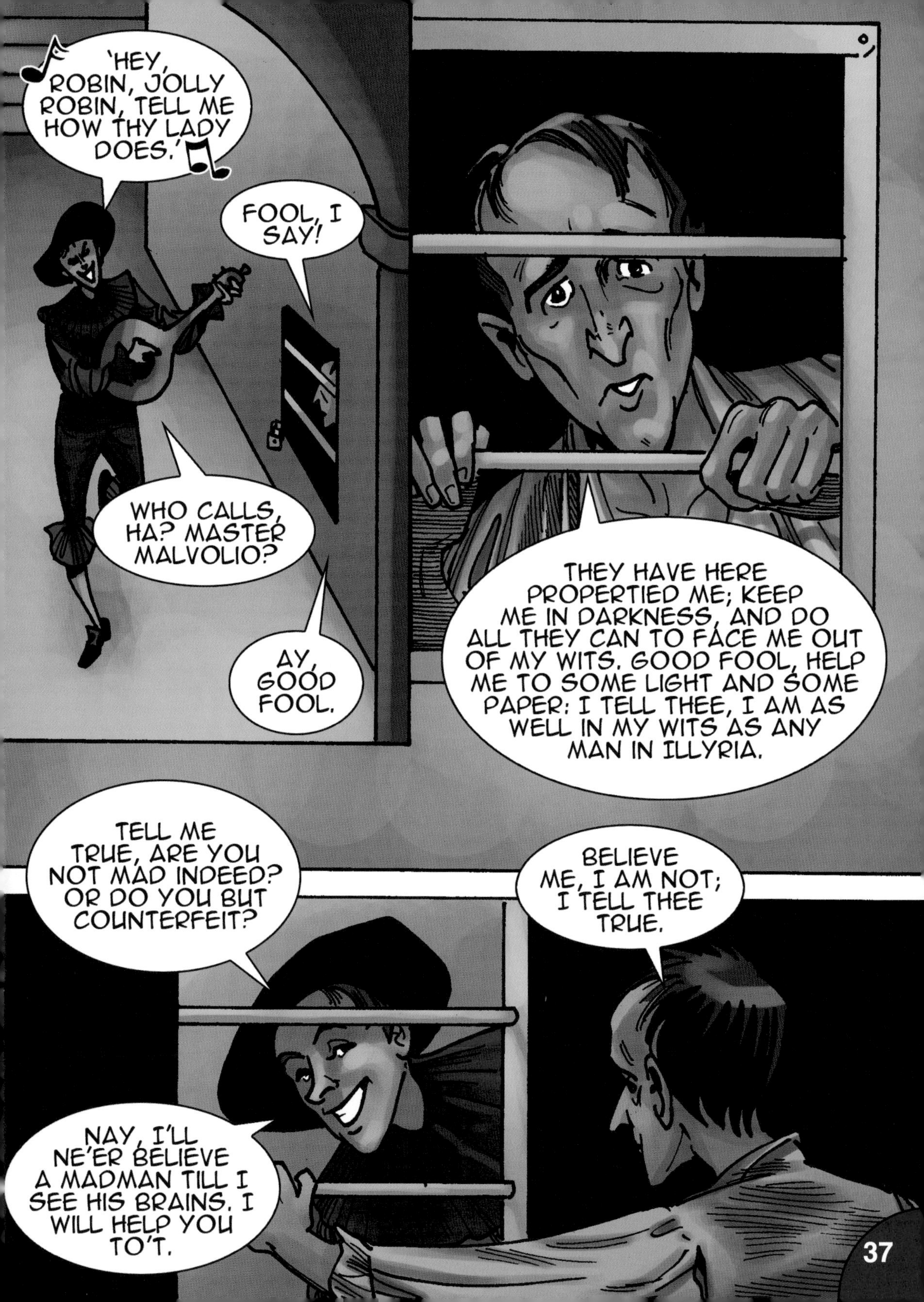
'HEY, ROBIN, JOLLY ROBIN, TELL ME HOW THY LADY DOES.'
FOOL, I SAY!
WHO CALLS, HA? MASTER MALVOLIO?
AY, GOOD FOOL.
THEY HAVE HERE PROPERTIED ME; KEEP ME IN DARKNESS, AND DO ALL THEY CAN TO FACE ME OUT OF MY WITS. GOOD FOOL, HELP ME TO SOME LIGHT AND SOME PAPER: I TELL THEE, I AM AS WELL IN MY WITS AS ANY MAN IN ILLYRIA.
TELL ME TRUE, ARE YOU NOT MAD INDEED? OR DO YOU BUT COUNTERFEIT?
BELIEVE ME, I AM NOT; I TELL THEE TRUE.
NAY, I'LL NE'ER BELIEVE A MADMAN TILL I SEE HIS BRAINS. I WILL HELP YOU TO'T.

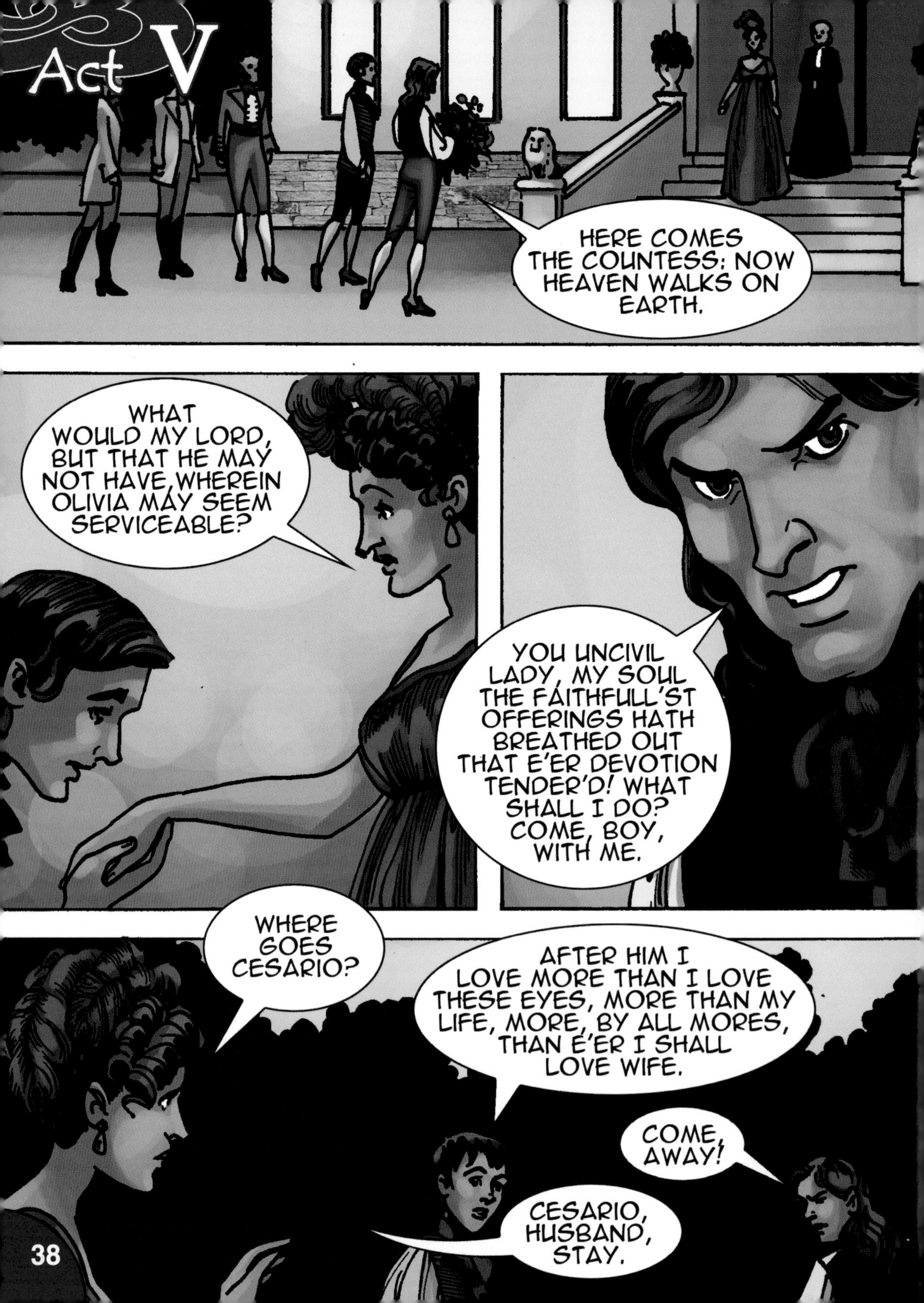
Act V
HERE COMES THE COUNTESS: NOW HEAVEN WALKS ON EARTH.
WHAT WOULD MY LORD, BUT THAT HE MAY NOT HAVE, WHEREIN OLIVIA MAY SEEM SERVICEABLE?
YOU UNCIVIL LADY, MY SOUL THE FAITHFULL'ST OFFERINGS HATH BREATHED OUT THAT E'ER DEVOTION TENDER'D! WHAT SHALL I DO? COME, BOY, WITH ME.
WHERE GOES CESARIO?
AFTER HIM I LOVE MORE THAN I LOVE THESE EYES, MORE THAN MY LIFE, MORE, BY ALL MORES, THAN E'ER I SHALL LOVE WIFE.
COME, AWAY!
CESARIO, HUSBAND, STAY.

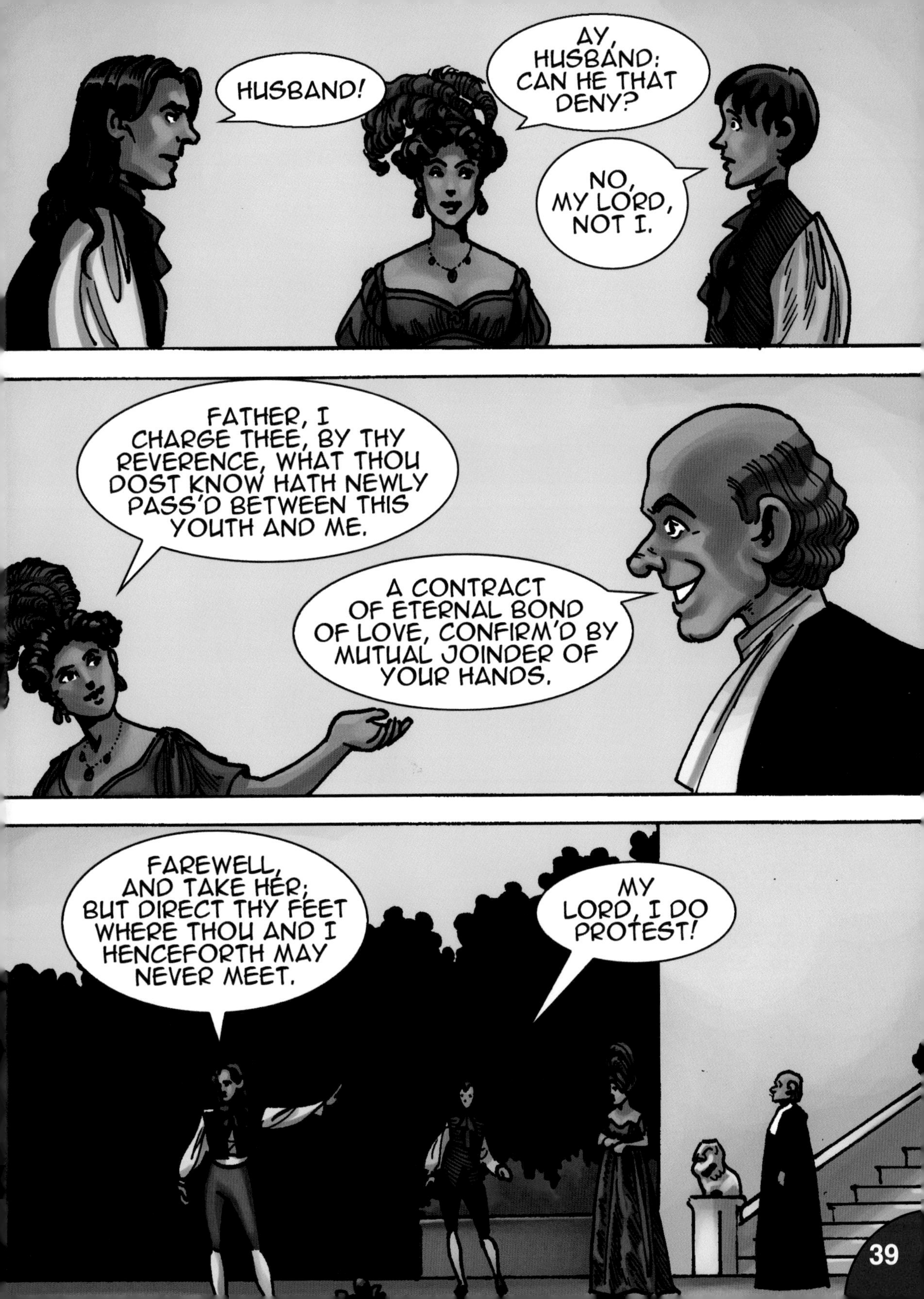
HUSBAND!
AY, HUSBAND: CAN HE THAT DENY?
NO, MY LORD, NOT I.
FATHER, I CHARGE THEE, BY THY REVERENCE, WHAT THOU DOST KNOW HATH NEWLY PASS'D BETWEEN THIS YOUTH AND ME.
A CONTRACT OF ETERNAL BOND OF LOVE, CONFIRM'D BY MUTUAL JOINDER OF YOUR HANDS.
FAREWELL, AND TAKE HER; BUT DIRECT THY FEET WHERE THOU AND I HENCEFORTH MAY NEVER MEET.
MY LORD, I DO PROTEST!

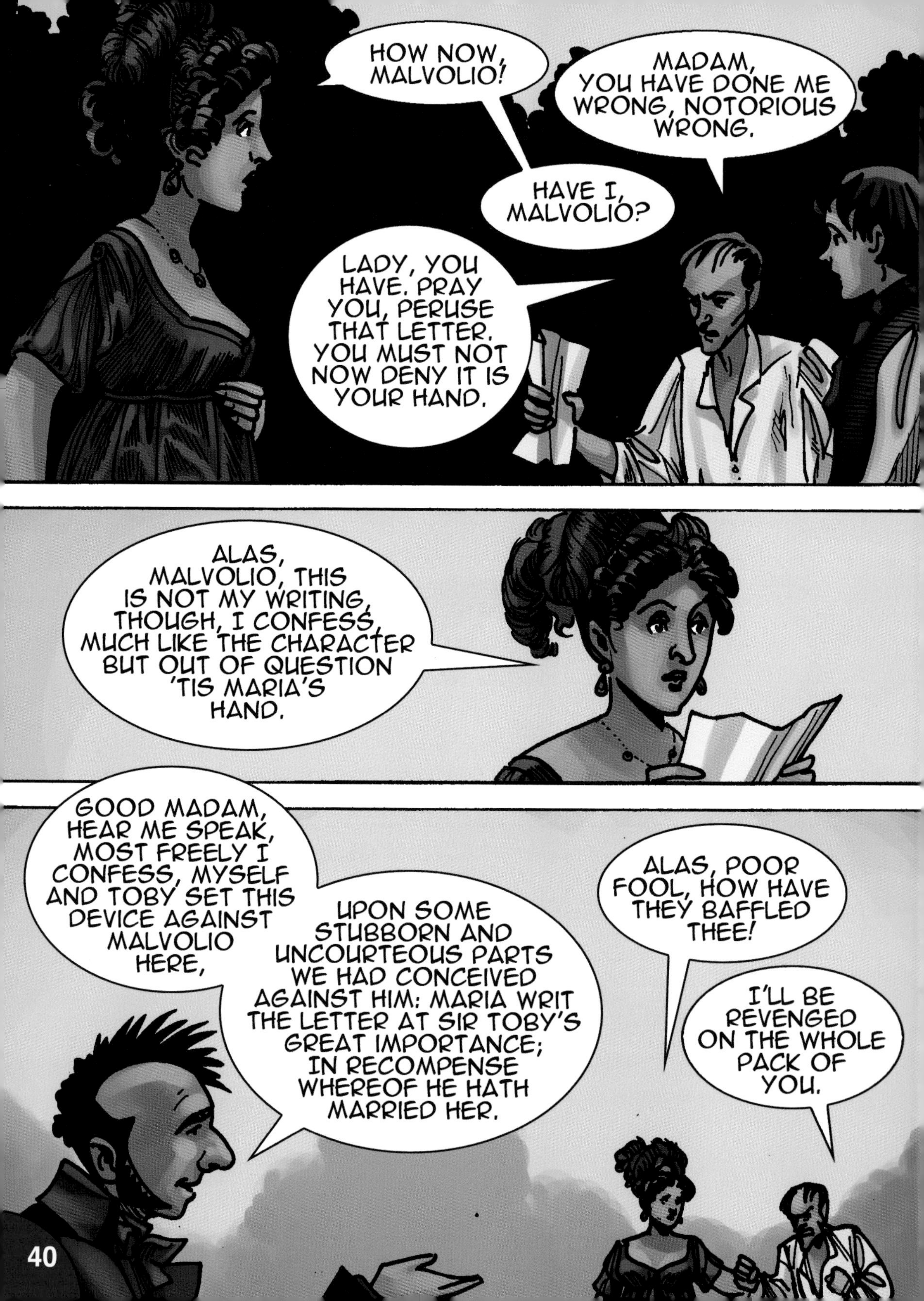
HOW NOW, MALVOLIO!
MADAM, YOU HAVE DONE ME WRONG, NOTORIOUS WRONG.
HAVE I, MALVOLIO?
LADY, YOU HAVE. PRAY YOU, PERUSE THAT LETTER. YOU MUST NOT NOW DENY IT IS YOUR HAND.
ALAS, MALVOLIO, THIS IS NOT MY WRITING, THOUGH, I CONFESS, MUCH LIKE THE CHARACTER BUT OUT OF QUESTION 'TIS MARIA'S HAND.
GOOD MADAM, HEAR ME SPEAK, MOST FREELY I CONFESS, MYSELF AND TOBY SET THIS DEVICE AGAINST MALVOLIO HERE,
UPON SOME STUBBORN AND UNCOURTEOUS PARTS WE HAD CONCEIVED AGAINST HIM: MARIA WRIT THE LETTER AT SIR TOBY'S GREAT IMPORTANCE; IN RECOMPENSE WHEREOF HE HATH MARRIED HER.
ALAS, POOR FOOL, HOW HAVE THEY BAFFLED THEE!
I'LL BE REVENGED ON THE WHOLE PACK OF YOU.

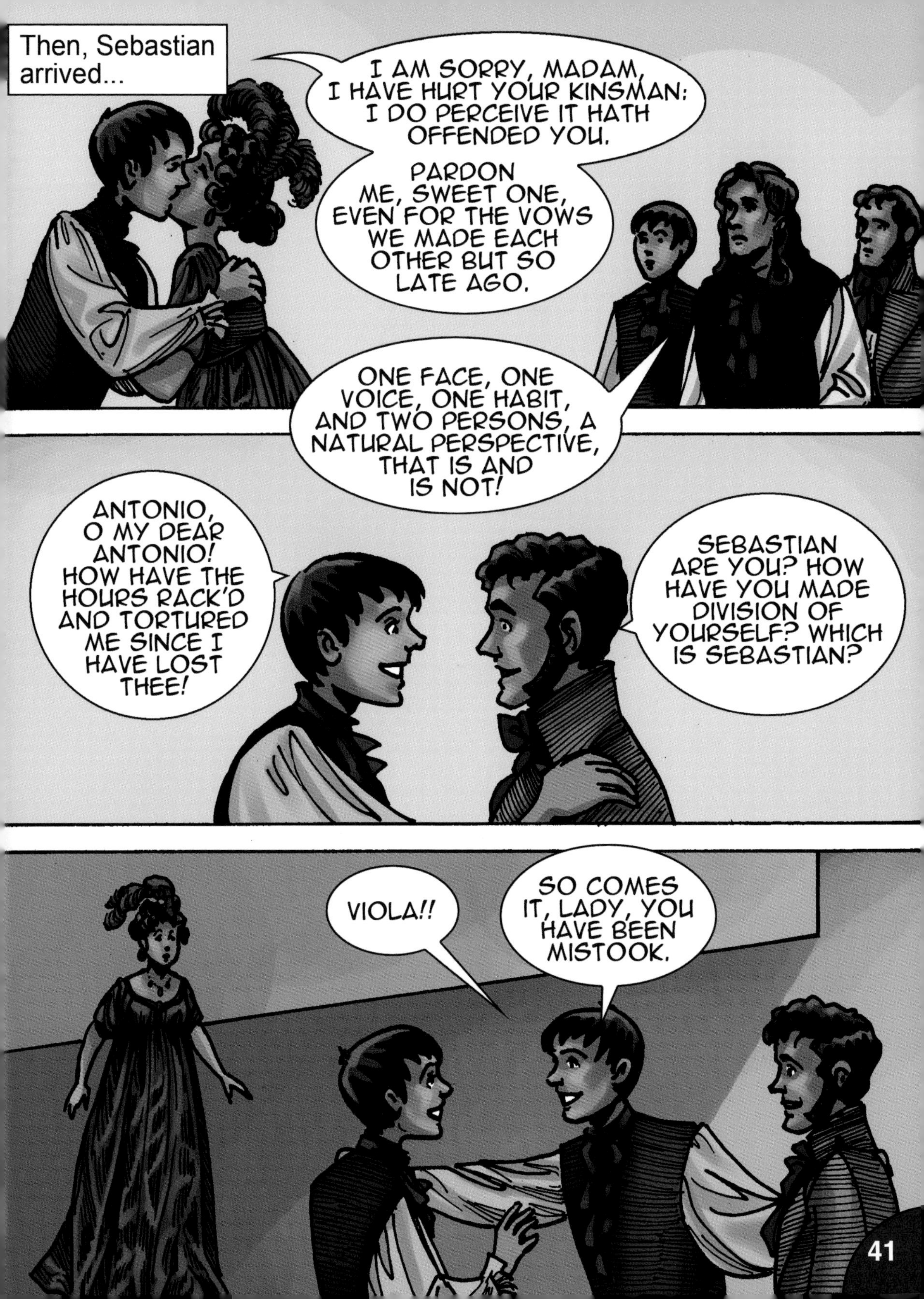
Then, Sebastian arrived...
I AM SORRY, MADAM, I HAVE HURT YOUR KINSMAN: I DO PERCEIVE IT HATH OFFENDED YOU.
PARDON ME, SWEET ONE, EVEN FOR THE VOWS WE MADE EACH OTHER BUT SO LATE AGO.
ONE FACE, ONE VOICE, ONE HABIT, AND TWO PERSONS, A NATURAL PERSPECTIVE, THAT IS AND IS NOT!
ANTONIO, O MY DEAR ANTONIO! HOW HAVE THE HOURS RACK'D AND TORTURED ME SINCE I HAVE LOST THEE!
SEBASTIAN ARE YOU? HOW HAVE YOU MADE DIVISION OF YOURSELF? WHICH IS SEBASTIAN?
VIOLA!!
SO COMES IT, LADY, YOU HAVE BEEN MISTOOK.

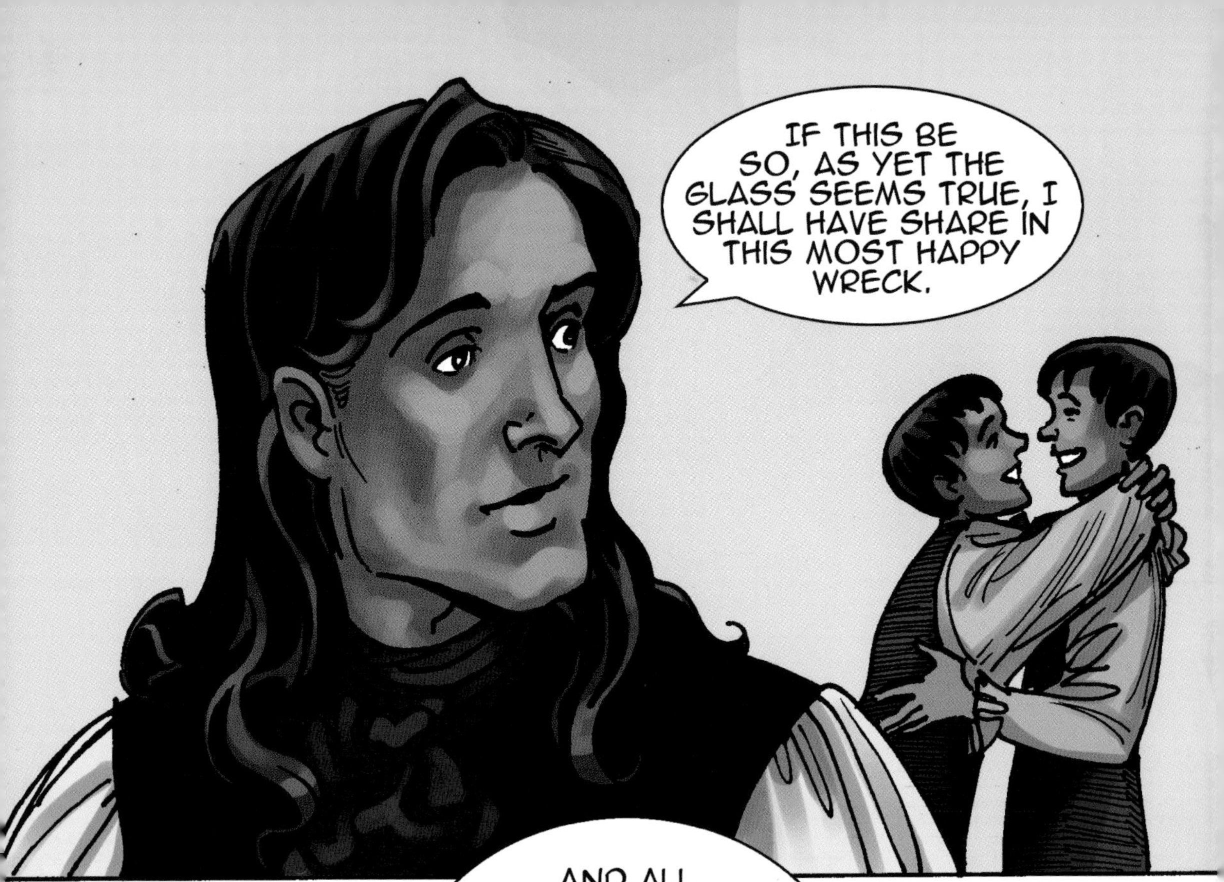
IF THIS BE SO, AS YET THE GLASS SEEMS TRUE, I SHALL HAVE SHARE IN THIS MOST HAPPY WRECK.

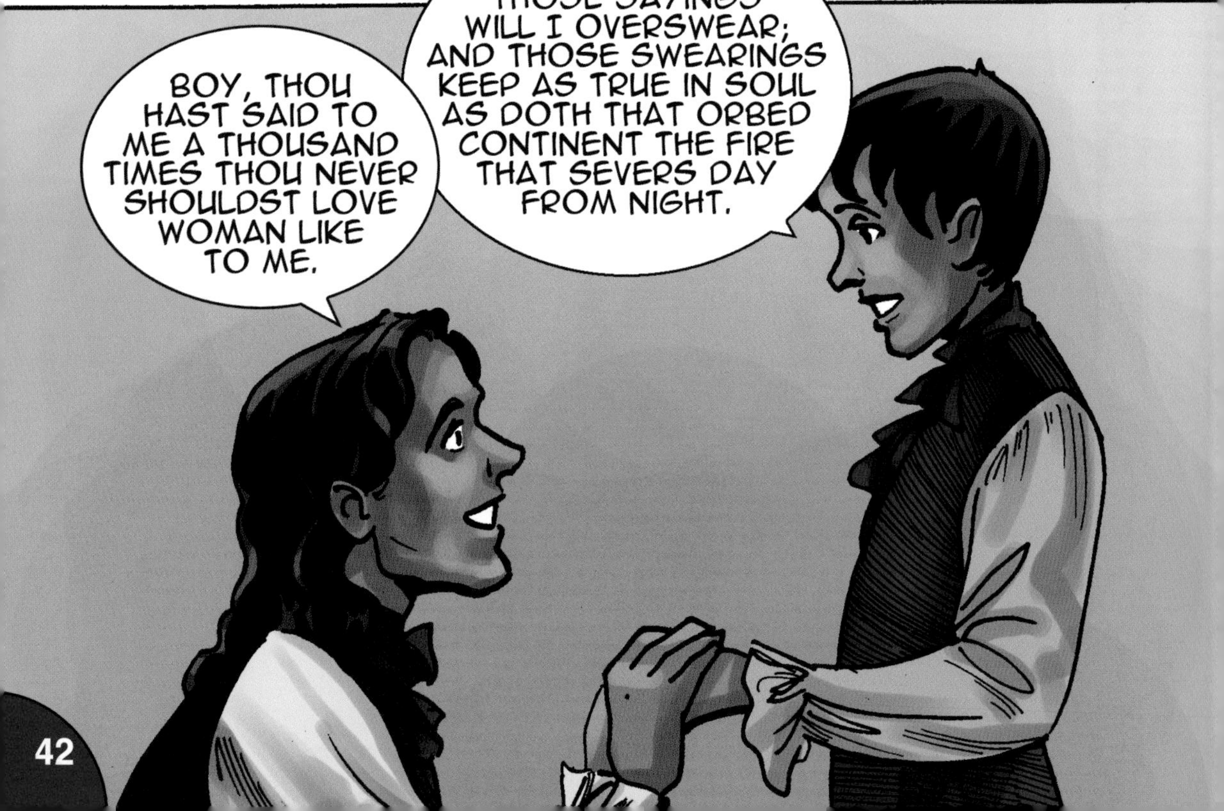
BOY, THOU HAST SAID TO ME A THOUSAND TIMES THOU NEVER SHOULDST LOVE WOMAN LIKE TO ME.
AND ALL THOSE SAYINGS WILL I OVERSWEAR; AND THOSE SWEARINGS KEEP AS TRUE IN SOUL AS DOTH THAT ORBED CONTINENT THE FIRE THAT SEVERS DAY FROM NIGHT.

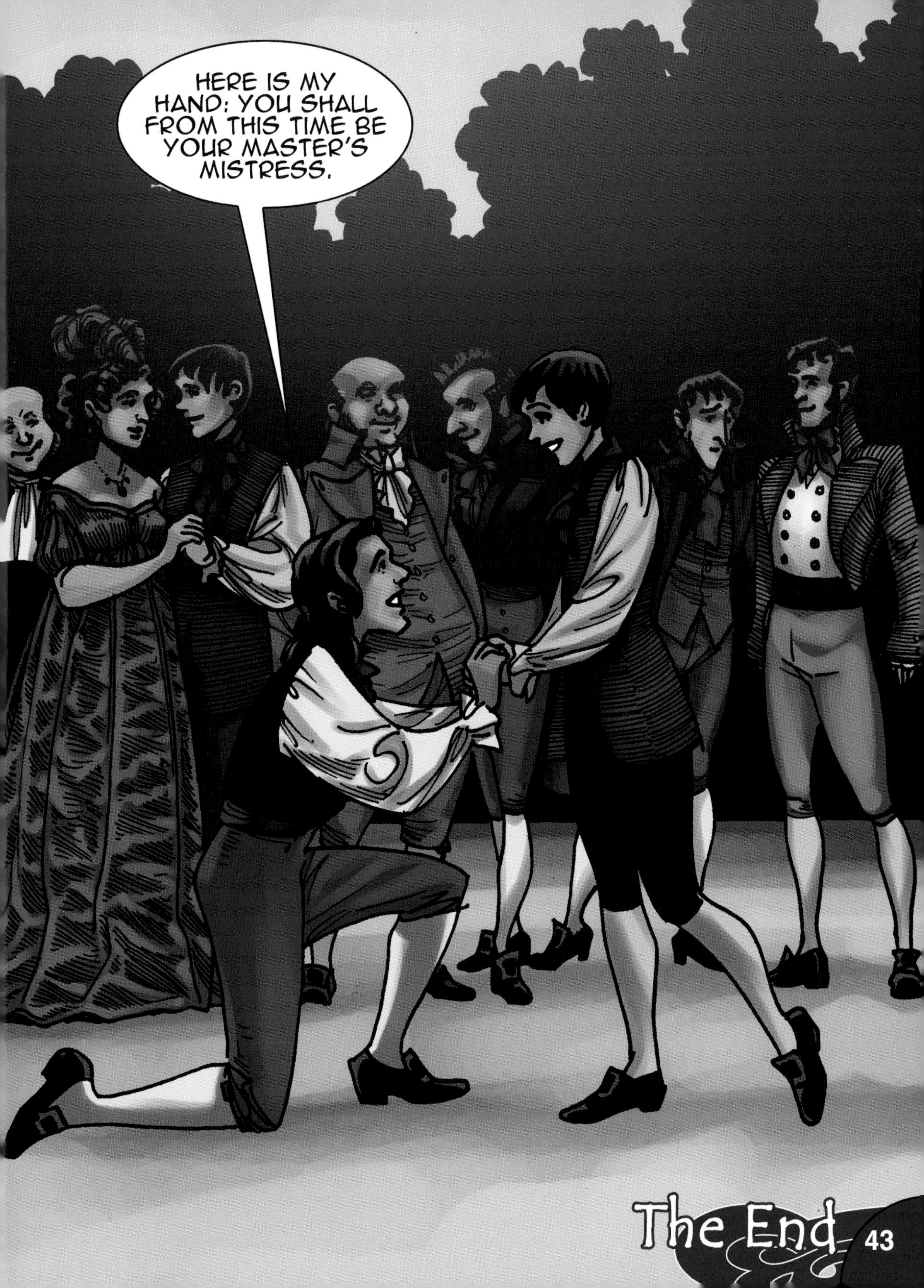
HERE IS MY HAND: YOU SHALL FROM THIS TIME BE YOUR MASTER'S MISTRESS.
The End

Behind Twelfth Night

Twelfth Night was written in about 1600 to 1602. It is part of Shakespeare's First Folio, which was printed in 1623. The full title of the five-act play is Twelfth Night, or, What You Will. This play is one of Shakespeare's best-known romantic comedies.

Shakespeare based his plots on historical and literary works, which was typical in his time. Twelfth Night is based on a story from Riche His Farewell to Military Profession, written by Barnabe Riche and published in 1581. Riche's story is based on an Italian comedy called Gl'ingannati, which was written and performed in 1531.

The plot of Twelfth Night revolves around a humorous love triangle and mistaken identities. In this play, identical twins Viola and Sebastian are separated after a shipwreck. Viola disguises herself as a man, Cesario, to work for Duke Orsino. The duke, who is in love with Olivia, sends Cesario to woo Olivia for him. Instead, Olivia falls in love with Cesario, who is in love with the duke.

Meanwhile, Sebastian arrives in Illyria. Olivia then meets Sebastian, who falls in love with her. She mistakes Sebastian for Cesario and marries him. After much comical confusion, Viola takes off her disguise and declares her love for the duke. Finally, Viola and the duke are married.

The first performance of *Twelfth Night* probably took place on the Christian festival known as Epiphany, or Twelfth Night. This festival is celebrated 12 days after Christmas. Since its beginning, *Twelfth Night* has been performed onstage throughout the world. There are also both film and television adaptations of this famous play.

Famous Phrases

If music be the food of love, play on.

Love sought is good, but given unsought is better.

Many a good hanging prevents a bad marriage.

Some are born great, some achieve greatness, and some have greatness thrust upon 'em.

About the Author

William Shakespeare was baptized on April 26, 1564, in Stratford-upon-Avon, England. At the time, records were not kept of births, however, the churches did record baptisms, weddings, and deaths. So, we know approximately when he was born. Traditionally, his birth is celebrated on April 23.

William was the son of John Shakespeare, a tradesman, and Mary Arden. He most likely attended grammar school and learned to read, write, and speak Latin.

Shakespeare did not go on to the university. Instead, he married Anne Hathaway at age 18. They had three children, Susanna, Hamnet, and Judith. Not much is known about Shakespeare's life at this time. By 1592 he had moved to London, and his name began to appear in the literary world.

In 1594, Shakespeare became an important member of Lord Chamberlain's company of players. This group had the best actors and the best theater, the Globe. For the next 20 years, Shakespeare devoted himself to writing. He died on April 23, 1616, but his works have lived on.

Additional Works by Shakespeare

The Comedy of Errors (1589–94)
The Taming of the Shrew (1590–94)
Romeo and Juliet (1594–96)
A Midsummer Night's Dream (1595–96)
Much Ado About Nothing (1598–99)
As You Like It (1598–1600)
Hamlet (1599–1601)
Twelfth Night (1600–02)
Othello (1603–04)
King Lear (1605–06)
Macbeth (1606–07)
The Tempest (1611)

About the Adapters

Cynthia Martin is one of the few women working in mainstream American comics. She worked for Marvel, pencilling and inking several titles such as *Star Wars*. She also drew for the comic series *Elvira*, based on the television show.

Vincent Goodwin earned his B.A. in Drama and Communications from Trinity University in San Antonio. He is the writer of three plays as well as the co-writer of the comic book *Pirates vs. Ninjas II*. Goodwin is also an accomplished journalist, having won several awards for his work as a columnist and reporter.

Glossary

adieu - a French word for "good-bye."

anon - right away.

beseech - to beg.

constellation - a person's nature, which was determined by the position of the stars at the time of his or her birth.

contempt - a lack of respect.

cross-gartered - a way of dressing where the garters cross in the back so they appear above and below the knee.

dormouse - sleepy.

fadge - to work out.

negligence - showing carelessness.

notorious - widely known and unliked.

perchance - by mere chance.

prithee - a way to make a request.

quaff - to drink deeply.

sanctity - being holy.

substractor - someone who speaks ill of another person.

Web Sites

To learn more about William Shakespeare, visit ABDO Publishing Company on the World Wide Web at **www.abdopublishing.com**. Web sites about Shakespeare are featured on our Book Links page. These links are routinely monitored and updated to provide the most current information available.